The Linden Tree

ALSO BY CÉSAR AIRA FROM NEW DIRECTIONS

Conversations

Dinner

Ema, the Captive

An Episode in the Life of a Landscape Painter

Ghosts

The Hare

How I Became a Nun

The Literary Conference

The Little Buddhist Monk and *The Proof*

The Miracle Cures of Dr. Aira

The Musical Brain

The Seamstress and the Wind

Shantytown

Varamo

The Linden Tree

•

CÉSAR AIRA

Translated by Chris Andrews

A NEW DIRECTIONS PAPERBOOK ORIGINAL

Manufactured in the United States of America
First published as a New Directions Paperbook (NDP1404) in 2018
New Directions books are published on acid-free paper
Design by Erik Rieselbach

Library of Congress Cataloging-in-Publication Data
Names: Aira, César, 1949– author. | Andrews, Chris, 1962– translator.
Title: The linden tree / César Aira ; translated from the Spanish by Chris Andrews.
Other titles: Tilo. English
Description: First American paperback edition. | New York, N.Y. : New Directions Publishing Corporation, 2018. | "A New Directions Paperbook Original." | "Originally published in Argentina as El tilo by Beatriz Viterbo Editora" — Verso title page.
Identifiers: LCCN 2017028331 | ISBN 9780811219082 (alk. paper)
Subjects: LCSH: Authors—Fiction. | Reminiscing—Fiction. | Childhood and youth—Fiction. | Autobiographical memory—Fiction. | Buenos Aires (Argentina)—Fiction. | Psychological fiction. | GSAFD: Autobiographical fiction.
Classification: LCC PQ7798.1.I7 T5513 2018 | DDC 863/.64—dc23
LC record available at https://lccn.loc.gov/2017028331

10 9 8 7 6 5 4 3 2 1

New Directions Books are published for James Laughlin
by New Directions Publishing Corporation
80 Eighth Avenue, New York 10011

THE LINDEN TREE

THE LINDEN IS A SMALL, ELEGANT TREE WITH A SLEN-der trunk, seemingly blessed with eternal youth. On the Plaza in Pringles, as well as ten thousand normal linden trees, there was also, by some strange quirk of Nature, one that had grown to an enormous size: it looked ancient, with its twisted trunk and impenetrable crown, and it was bigger than twenty of the others put together. I nicknamed it the Monster Linden Tree. I regarded it with a certain awe, or respect at least, but also with affection, because like all trees it was harmless. No one had seen such a big linden tree anywhere else, and we thought of it as a monument to the singularity of our town. It was an aberration, but superb, with all the exotic majesty of the unique and the unrepeatable.

My father, who suffered from chronic insomnia, would go to the Plaza with a bag at the beginning of summer to collect the linden's little flowers, which he then dried and used to make a tea that he drank at night, after dinner. The linden's calm-ing properties are universally acknowledged, but I'm not sure that they reside in the flowers, which grow in little bunches and are yellow in color, barely distinct from the green of the leaves. I seem to remember that the flowers close to form a fruit, which is like a little Gothic capsule. Or maybe it's the other

way around: the capsule comes first and opens into a flower ...
Memory might be playing tricks on me ... It would be easy to
clear this up, because linden trees haven't changed, and here
in Flores, where I live, there are plenty that I could inspect.
I haven't (which shows how totally unscientific I am), but it
doesn't matter. I can't remember if my father used the flowers or the leaves or the little capsules; no doubt he did it in his
own special way, as he did everything else. Perhaps he had discovered how to extract the maximum benefit from the linden's
well-known calming properties; if so, I have reason to regret my
distraction and poor memory, because whatever the recipe or
method was, it died with him.

It might also be that the natural processes of flowering and
fruiting had undergone some transformation in that unique
specimen that grew on the Plaza in Pringles: the Monster Linden Tree. That was the tree from which my father took his har-
vest; he considered it lucky. No other substance in the universe,
he claimed, not even the powerful sedatives used to commit
suicide, could have sent him to sleep like that linden blossom
tea. If its powers were due to a genetic mutation of the Monster
Linden Tree, my efforts to remember his method are pointless,
because there would be no way to source the key ingredient.

Writing this now, I realize that all these years I too have be-
lieved implicitly in the effectiveness of the beverage, but not because of any solid evidence: it might have worked like a placebo
on my father's system because of his belief (which I have inherited); or perhaps it didn't work at all. Nothing is more con-

troversial than the action of psychotropic substances, whether natural or synthetic.

There is no way for me to verify the special calming properties of the Monster Linden Tree because it no longer exists; it was cut down in an irrational act of political hatred, the final act of a legendary local drama whose central figure was the Peronist Boy. One night, the boy took refuge at the top of the tree, and a band of furious fanatics who were pursuing him hacked at its trunk with axes ... The boy, who was my age, so I can fully identify with him, became a symbol, for family reasons. "The Peronist Boy": how absurd! Children can't be identified politically; they don't belong to the left or the right. He wouldn't have understood what he was representing. The symbol had infected him like a fateful virus. But it's true that childhood, as reflection or analogy, can stand for anything. And Perón himself promoted the idea that the evolution of society would necessarily produce Peronist children: there was a biology of Peronism.

The strangest thing was that the band pursuing him was a commando unit of the Peronist Resistance, led by Ciancio, the mattress maker. A complex series of misunderstandings had led them to misread the (positive or negative) "coefficient" of the symbolism conveyed by the boy. This suggests the complexity of our political quarrels, which later simplification has tried to reduce to black and white.

That cruel midnight, the sound of the axe-blows went on and on, like a terrifying tom-tom ... I said that I was the same age as the boy, and nothing could prove it better than this: the only book that I had as a child, or the only one I remember, was *Sambo*, a lovely little volume whose pages, instead of being rectangular like those of other books were cut into the shape of a tree (what wouldn't I give to have it now!). The Peronist Boy must have had that book too, or he must have seen it, because it was very popular at the time, I don't know why. Sambo, the little black boy, hid from the tigers in the top of a tree, and the tigers came and circled around the base until they melted into butter, as I remember. The Peronist Boy translated the fable into reality, although in its symbolic way the story remained an animal fable. After all, weren't the anti-Peronists called gorillas? And gorillas build their nests in trees, don't they?

Axe-blows, and midnight's dome over the Plaza, with its dark ecliptics tracing interplanetary routes to all the nameless horrors of life, to all the figures that would one day come to be art. To other worlds, worlds in reverse, where Peronists and anti-Peronists changed places.

Since then, whenever I put my ear to the pillow, I hear those tom-tom blows in the darkness; not that I could actually hear the axe at the time, except in the stories that my mother told me about the events of that night. I now know that what I have been hearing all these years is the pulsing of my blood, but it makes no difference; the pulses still symbolize that threat ... So I have to change position and lie on my back, which is uncomfortable and keeps me awake. This is the cause of my cruel insomnia, which leaves me feeling that life is unbearable.

Although these events have been adorned, deformed, and enveloped in the prestige of legend, they really happened. It's hard to believe—they seem made up—and yet they happened, and I was there, not at the top of the tree, but there in those days, in that town, in that world, which is now so far away. My whole life has taken on the unreal color of that fable; since then I have never been able to find a footing in reality.

Books, art, travel, love, all the hackneyed wonders of the universe have served as multicolored distractions from that legend and everything that floated in the dark sea over the Monster Linden Tree. I have used them to sublimate my lack of a real life ... and have even come to think of myself as privileged. But the disappearance of that giant therapeutic tree from the symbolic system has had its effects. The nervous disposition that I have inherited is a torment: there is a vibration at the center of my being and when it reaches my skin (as it does constantly, because it never goes away, not even for a minute), the anxiety that it provokes is larger than thought itself ... and I feel that I can't go on living ... I think about death, which, given my nature, is the last thing I should be thinking about. Inevitably, I have sought relief in alcohol and drugs, especially alcohol, which breaks over me like a wave of despair ... Getting out of bed in the small hours, unable to withstand the anxiety a moment longer, wandering around the dark apartment until I confirm once again, as every night, that there is no getting away from it. Death is no solution because my corpse would get up too ... What can I do? It's beyond my control, I can't help it ...

There must be some active principle in linden blossom tea if my father went on drinking it, religiously, every night for all those years. And he clearly needed it, for he was the most excitable of men. Behind his back, my mother used to call him "Live Wire," or "Boilinmilk," the name of a character in a funny cartoon strip. Because as well as being excitable, he was extremely quick-tempered, always about to fly off the handle, a powder keg. All it took was a word, an expression, and he would be shouting like a furious madman. Much less than that, in fact, could make him lose control. He had magically refined the causes: the flapping of a butterfly's wings in Japan could bring on one of his attacks in Pringles. He was perpetually wound up, wired: eyes flashing, lips trembling, hair bristling, the veins almost popping out of his neck, limbs in constant agitation, his torso continually swiveling this way and that, as if he were inhabited by an animal on the lookout for enemies. My father's enemies were imaginary, or rather his enemy was the world; or, to resort to a commonplace, he was his own worst enemy.

I don't know how intentional this was, but I notice that a couple of metaphors from a branch of applied physics (electricity) found their way into the previous paragraph. They are apt, not because of my descriptive powers or my (deficient) literary skill, but because of an incidental fact: my father was an electrician by trade. Sometimes it happens that way: an "electric" man is an electrician. It happens especially in small towns, where everyone knows everyone else, and these "real jokes" become a conversation topic and constitute a kind of traditional lore, handed down from generation to generation. I remember at some point feeling proud to have a famous father; I think it was the only time there seemed to be anything positive about his terrible nerves, which made daily life such a minefield. Later on, I would change my mind and come to hate those small-town reputations, when I discovered their unpleasant tendency to encourage embellishment: gossips can't resist adding to them, giving the victim a reputation for something else, and something else again, for no other reason than to pass the time and exercise their malevolence. It's a well-known mechanism and by no means limited to small towns: reputations grow, and since they need to be fed with new material, invention becomes inevitable.

But my father had a certain right to notoriety, prior to the electric-electrician coincidence. History is crucial here, so I should give some dates to make myself clear. I was born in 1949, at the climax of the Peronist regime. My parents weren't very young; I wasn't one of those automatic children of the proletariat, born out of biological necessity as soon as their progenitors emerge from childhood themselves. In my case, there was family planning, as indicated by the fact that I was an only child. All my friends in the neighborhood were only children too: we were the generation—produced, precisely, by the Peronist social laws—with which the idea of ascending to the middle class lodged itself in proletarian minds. The first step in this project was to keep reproduction within the bounds of affordability. There was, however, a limit to this rationalism, namely that everyone wanted a boy; so that if the first child had turned out to be a girl, they would have been prepared to shoulder the burden and try again. I'm using the conditional because this didn't actually happen: they all had a boy first off and then stopped. There was something magical about Peronism, something like wish fulfillment. Psychic predisposition might also have played a role: they say that something similar happens when there's a war; and maybe back then, in Peronist eternity, the deep layers of the popular mind could already intuit the wars to come.

When I say, "They all had a boy ...," I'm exaggerating, of course. That was what I saw around me, but my experience was very limited. With time, I began to realize that there were girls as well, although I had failed to notice them in the bewilderment of early childhood, with its anxious choosing of friends, its initiatory games and adventures. Then a curious fact made them all the more conspicuous: there was never just one girl, or a girl with brothers; there were always three of them, three little sisters one after the other. This was because the couples whose firstborn child had been a girl tried again, and when they had a second girl, they took another chance ... But they stopped after three, because it would have been crazy to go on ... And that was how the poor neighborhoods of Pringles came to have their curious demography: a large majority of families with one boy, and a few families here and there with three girls. There were no cases of mixed offspring. There was something magical about Peronism, but it was an implacable magic. Or perhaps Nature activated some mysterious safeguard, intervening in History to protect the species.

My father was a staunch Peronist from way back, right from the start, I suppose. And for him, as for so many Argentinians of modest means, it paid off: in his case, not just via the labor laws, the social benefits, and the hope of betterment that spread throughout society, but individually too, because his loyalty was rewarded with a lucrative council job. During the ten years of the regime, he was in charge of the electrical systems for the lighting of the streets and public buildings. A role of great responsibility, as you can imagine; it's really quite amazing that it could have been fulfilled by one man, even though Pringles was (and remains) a small town. I should point out that my father wasn't responsible for the supply of electricity to the community: the Electricity Plant, also called (I don't know why) the Electricity Cooperative, took care of that. As I reconstruct the situation now, I presume that the bulk of his work—apart from odd trips to the courthouse or the post office or the library to change a bulb or fluorescent tube or to fix a short circuit—consisted in looking after the street lighting. The town was about fifteen blocks by fifteen, and there was a lamp hanging exactly at the center of each intersection. There was also the long boulevard that led to the station, and the path to the cemetery. And the Plaza, of course. It was no small task for just one man, without any helpers. I was too young in 1955, when my father stopped doing that job, to remember how he organized his time, but I bet he had it all worked out and got it done with time to spare. Life was simpler back then, and electrical systems were rudimentary, straight from the textbook, with the causes and effects on display.

The earliest memory that I have of my father is of him riding the bicycle that he used for getting all around town, even to its farthest limits, carrying a very long ladder on his shoulder. I don't think this scene would have stuck in my mind without its most salient feature: the ladder. It was a wooden ladder, at least four yards long (I don't want to exaggerate), and balancing such a cumbersome piece of equipment while riding a bike must have required a certain skill, or at least regular practice. If my father ever fell off, or had an accident, he didn't mention it at home.

I discovered all this much later, actually, after the demise of Peronism, when my family, along with so many others, had fallen back to its fated place. I found out almost by guesswork, starting from those dubious memories of early childhood. Are they memories or inventions? You can never really know. I had to guess, because at home we never spoke of the past. The Revolución Libertadora brought down an impenetrable curtain, woven from threads of the shameful dream of becoming middle class, a dream that turned out, on waking, to be as indecent as a sexual fantasy. Also, it would have been awkward to talk about that past because the word "Perón" had been prohibited by decree, and the prohibition was respected even in the privacy of the home. My parents never spoke that word again. No one did, and I wonder how I even knew that it existed. Naturally I had often heard it during the first six years of my life, and its subsequent elimination (I didn't speak it either, not even mentally) gave it a special place. The elimination was so complete that I distinctly remember the first time I heard it, many years later, when I was finishing primary school: a girl from my class said, "Perón ..." I felt as if an abyss had opened and was swallowing up my whole life. It's inexplicable, although there must be some explanation. Of course it was possible to go on talking without using that word; its absence was not an obstacle to communication in daily life, because it wasn't the name of something that we might have needed to mention: it was a proper name, belonging to just one thing in the universe.

Although this elimination took place in every home in the country, in mine it had a precedent that made it more logical, or perhaps overdetermined it. This was something that happened before the Revolución Libertadora, so for me it is even farther back in the mists of early childhood. When I began to find out about it, much later on, it came as a surprise, and I couldn't retrieve any memory to confirm the events in question. It turned out that in his youth my father had been a fervent Catholic. More than that, actually: he was fanatical, daily mass and daily communion, a true believer, a soldier in the legions of Our Lady ... but after the events of 1954, when Perón broke with the clergy, never, not once in the rest of his days, did my father set foot in a church again. Strange as it may seem, in the conflict of loyalties between Christianity and Peronism, the second won out. If churches had been burned in Pringles as they were in Buenos Aires, he would have been there with a torch. Nine out of ten people would condemn this as retrospective hypocrisy, but I think I understand it, insofar as something so deeply strange can be understood. You have to bear in mind that in Argentina, as opposed to other Latin American countries, Catholicism never took root in the working class. It was always the prerogative of "respectable" people and fundamentally, I would say, of the highest strata of society: the agnostic middle class participated in the rituals out of respect for the patricians, or out of snobbery, to distinguish themselves from the dark and decidedly atheist masses. Which meant that my father's devout faith had been a complete anomaly and could only have been sincere. But he was a Peronist first: he had to choose and he chose Peronism. And the fact that he chose, rather than seeking a compromise or turning a blind eye, is irrefutable proof of his sincerity.

Perhaps I can make this clearer by explaining how I found out. It was, as I said, many years later; I must have been a teenager. One day, by chance, I overheard two ladies from the neighborhood who were sitting in a parked truck having a conversation. This might seem odd, but a lot of truck drivers lived in that part of town, and they left their vehicles parked in the street in front of their houses; in the afternoon, the women would often adjourn to the cabins to knit and chat. It was one of the local customs. Those cabins were fine observation posts— elevated, warm, protected by glass—and the ladies made the most of them while their husbands or sons were asleep, having driven through the night. I had climbed up into the back of the truck, as I often did, and that's how I heard them. I wasn't really paying attention; I was trying not to make a noise and give myself away as I played my solitary games, fantasizing about voyages and wars. I was listening just enough to make sure that they hadn't noticed the presence of an intruder. "Black scum!" said one to the other. "Once I saw him in the Chapel of the Immaculate Conception ... He went to all the churches, he was always in one or another ... I was at the back and I saw him from behind, kneeling in front of a saint, praying and praying, hanging his head, then he lit a candle, prayed some more, beat his breast, went to another saint, did the same thing, and kissed the foot of the statue. Then he went to a Virgin, and then to another, kissed the hem of her robe, knelt down again, touched the floor with his forehead ... I was thinking, 'Who *is* this? Where did this guy come from?' Until he turned around and I saw his face ... It was him! What a creep!" The other one chimed in: "They're the worst." And the first lady, remembering another detail: "Ah yes, and every time he stepped into the aisle he crossed himself, not with a simple sign of the cross, but the complete works, making a little cross on his forehead ..." "Oh yes, like that," said the other, disgusted not by the sign but by my father's fanatical, meticulous piety. "What an incense-sniffer ..."

I imagine my father in that dark, empty chapel, thinking that he was alone and unobserved, in a paroxysm of faith. Or I try to but can't. I mean: I can see him, like a cutout figure, a puppet on a string, performing his liturgical dance, but I simply can't imagine what was going through his mind at that moment, what he was asking of the saints and the Virgins, why it was so important to him ... Although it should be possible to get *some* idea, now. I was less struck by the ladies' derogatory comments than by the scene that one of them had evoked. Spite was nothing new to me; it was almost a way of life. My mother's tongue was sharp enough ... I felt that I could translate what they had said into political terms. "They're the worst" meant "the Peronists." What they objected to was a poor electrician, and especially one with "connections," taking on the attributes of a mystic. Those ladies would not have been overly shocked, if at all, when the Peronists started burning churches later on. But the mere idea of a Peronist being a disgusting incense-sniffer ... I contented myself with that explanation and sought no further. Nevertheless, there was something that didn't quite fit, a loose end that bothered me: that affected piety, those gesticulations before the altar, the candles, the novenas to Our Lady—there was something inescapably feminine about it all. And my father was very virile: if there was one quality that he possessed beyond all doubt, that was it. So there remained the shadow of a contradiction, which could only be resolved by a synthetic term at a higher level, which for the moment eluded me ... But it must have been lying dormant somewhere in my brain, preparing me for future revelations.

"They're the worst ...": that little sentence said it all, and simply by hearing it that afternoon, I had, at some level, understood everything. The processes of my life and intellectual maturation continued, and it would be impossible for me to specify the precise moment at which I grasped the knowledge in a concrete way, but this impossibility stems not so much from the difficulty of reconstructing history in detail as from the nature of knowledge itself. At what point do we understand that two and two make four? Although we might pinpoint the first time that someone told us this, or the first time we verified it by counting on our fingers, that would not give us the date. Because from much earlier on, from the beginning of life, we have seen two things here and another two there, or one thing and another, or two and one, or three and one, or one and one and one, or any number of other combinations, which, although they produced different results, were demonstrating the same mechanism. The consciously formulated proposition, "Two plus two equals four," does no more than gather up all these preparatory, isolated instances and tie them into a mnemonic knot.

"They're the worst" means adultery. Spoken by two ladies knitting in a parked truck, there's nothing else it can mean. I discovered this later, but I knew it all along. I don't think it ever felt like a revelation. Even if I had never heard the word "adultery," or the word "bigamy," I must have been aware of the thing. Words, in fact, are incidental; they are formulae for remembering things; we manipulate them in combinations that give us an illusion of power, but the things were there first, intractably.

Anyway, the story, or rather the legend (because it was never verified), was that my father had another woman, on the other side of town. More than that: another family, children, a house … This is a difficult subject for me but I have to admit that things could have been worse, because in small towns every story is surrounded by a constellation of causes and plausible explanations, unlike big-city stories, which are abrupt and often inexplicable. But here I can give only a cursory sketch of that constellation.

I should begin by pointing out two of my father's attributes, one positive and the other negative, from the town's point of view. The negative attribute was that his skin and hair were dark: he was "black" as they said back then; he probably had some Indian ancestry, but since the Indians in Argentina have always been seen as remote in time and space, that color was associated instead with poverty, servitude, ignorance, and the ranches. He never mentioned his background; I don't even know the names of my grandparents, or uncles and aunts, if I had any. In any case, history was superfluous: his appearance said it all. The positive attribute was that he was an extremely handsome and well-built man. Although it was very obvious, this physical beauty was completely canceled out by the social stigma of his color. It was perfectly possible for "blacks" to be more or less handsome, more or less ugly, but it was like saying that some dwarfs were taller or shorter than others: they were still dwarfs.

This duality might help to explain his marriage. My mother

was white; she came from a respectable, middle-class family, and if she had acquiesced to an alliance with the "black" populace, it was because her physical deformity made it impossible for her to marry at her own level. The alternative would have been to remain unmarried, and as far back as I can remember, she was always expressing her horror at the condition of the "spinster." In fact, she conducted a permanent campaign, a one-woman cold war against all spinsters: it was as if she saw them as a crime against humanity, and in the end humanity incorporated blacks as well as whites.

My father found himself in an unstable position: he had a legitimate, upwardly mobile family, with a single child—a nicely dressed boy, attending school—and a wife whose parents were European immigrants ... but he was "black." The blackness was irremediable, and it was intensified by the enigma of his beauty. There is something I should clarify here: it's inconceivable to me that the ladies in our social milieu could have appreciated his beauty, which was subsumed by the social misfortune of blackness, and yet they can't have failed to see it, if only as a mystery. In that other, alien world, where everyone was black, the differences must have been noticeable; they must have produced effects. So they were obliged to imagine that he had an escape valve, in the form of another woman, one from his own milieu, with whom he could have an indefinite number of children (as many as Nature ordained) and live in a manner befitting his condition. (There, in the other house, he didn't suffer from nervous tension; he was the very soul of serenity.)

As I said, I'm not sure whether this story belongs to the domain of logical constructions or to that of reality. But reality itself is a logical construction, the model for all the others, so it doesn't make much difference. My mother must have suffered greatly. Over the years, little by little, she shut herself into her suffering, withdrawing to a world apart, with its own peculiar laws. But she was not aware of this, and since she was a very sociable and curious woman, she went on interacting with the neighbors. The situation was made even stranger by her straightforwardness: she didn't have trouble with her nerves, or with anything, actually. She didn't seem to have secrets: she said whatever crossed her mind, however hurtful or embarrassing it might be for her interlocutors. My father used to warn me: "Your mother can't hold her tongue." And it was true, although in my innocence I didn't see it that way.

It's clear that my father had an institutionally structured mind: he was devoted to the Catholic Church and the Peronist regime. Outside of the institutions, he was neither one thing nor the other. I never saw him pray at home or even look at a religious image. As soon as he stopped going to church, he stopped being a Catholic, and maybe he stopped believing as well. As soon as the regime fell, he forgot about politics forever.

A kind of fable, just the one, survived from his time as official electrician. It wasn't nostalgia for economic prosperity but something much more poetic: the strange and slightly magical honor of having been responsible for switching on the lights in all the streets of the town. I always knew this; he didn't have to tell me. And I was not backward in telling my friends: "Before," my father had been the one who switched on the streetlights, all of them, even the farthest, the ones we never saw ... "Before." I didn't go into details about when this had been. In a way it suited me that the privilege belonged to another time: it added mystery. As night was beginning to fall, we would see the lights come on at the street corners, on their own, it seemed, as if a benevolent deity had said from afar, "It is time," but it was always a different time, because there in the south the seasonal differences are vast. The switches must have been in the town hall, or at the plant, and to me it was a wonder that they could send the blessing of light, by remote control, all through the town.

People didn't take electricity for granted back then in Pringles, not as they do now, anyway. The town depended on the countryside, and in the country most people lived without electricity. All our neighbors in town were country people, more or less, and they could appreciate that miracle for what it was truly worth. You didn't have to go far to see the difference: the electricity supply covered only the built-up area; it didn't extend to the dirt roads of the outskirts. The street where we lived was right on the edge of the grid: the people who lived behind us didn't have access to that privilege of civilization; that's how limited it was. In fact, we all had lamps from the preelectricity days. The queen of those devices was the famous Petromax, or Night Sun, which many people still preferred to electric light. They were used on patios, in sheds, or extensions that hadn't been wired. Also, there wasn't nearly as much electrical equipment as today. So-called "domestic appliances" were rare. Even a fridge was an exotic luxury: we never had one, for example; nor did anyone in the neighborhood, as far as I know. The only practical benefit of electricity was light, and that's what we called it: "the light."

After 1955, my father went on practicing his trade as an electrician, privately. He must have had his clients; he kept going out on his bicycle, though hardly ever with the ladder. No doubt there was a stressful transition, while he worked out how to get by without the salary. But I didn't notice: at the age of six, I would have been too preoccupied with my first year of school, and I don't think I was deprived of anything. Still, my parents must have felt that they had been wise not to have more children.

A child's father is a model, a mirror, and a hope. More than that, he's a typical man, a specimen of fully formed, adult humanity. A kind of Adam constructed from all the fragments of the world that the child progressively comes to know. It's hardly surprising that some parts don't fit and the whole turns out to be rather mysterious. The father is like a big, complex riddle whose answers appear one by one over the course of the child's life. I would even venture to say that those answers are our instructions for living. "What about people who don't have a father?" somebody might ask. But to that I can reply: Everyone has a father.

This leads to what has been, for me, one of the most haunt-

ing mysteries: Was my father a good electrician? Or was he simply incompetent? The maximal hypothesis, which I have enter-
tained at length, is that he knew nothing of the trade, not even
the basics. This would have meant that his whole existence
was a perilous kind of playacting. Faced with a plug, a cable, a
bulb, he would have wondered: What's this? And, obliged to do
something with that unknown quantity in order to justify his
role, he would have done some random thing, to see what happened … But no, it's impossible. I can't really believe it, whatever blandishments a teasing demon deploys to lure me in that
direction. No one could stake their destiny on such a complete
negation. And anyway, it would have been unsustainable: in all
those years of plying the trade, he must have learned *something*.

It's a fantasy; that's all it could be. Although there are cases
in which the best way to find an explanation is to begin by con-
sidering the most extreme hypothesis and then pull back to
reach the "happy medium" that so often corresponds to reality. Like everybody else, my father must have gotten it right on
some occasions and wrong on others. But various convergent
signs, as well as an ineffable but unerring intuition, lead me to
suppose that the second case was more frequent than the first.
Clients came back with complaints; problems became chronic;
he refused to work for certain people or kept putting them off.
He always seemed very confident, which in itself, as a blanket
policy, is a sure sign of his doubts. But the surest indication of
all, the infallible test, is the way things worked out in the end.
Taking the long view, it's clear that my father never got beyond

the level of the neighborhood handyman, doing odd jobs for
poor people: he didn't progress from repairs and tinkering to
installing built-in electrical systems. His glory days were behind him, and I have to concede that there may have been some
truth to what the "gorillas" supposed, hateful though it is: that
he had gotten his official job because of his Peronism (not his
skill as an electrician). If so, if he was a bungler, making it up
as he went along, it was all the more heroic; and had he—un-
imaginably—confessed, I would have loved him more.

The mysteries and secrets of the Electricity Fairy. Enig-
matic, hence dangerous. People were said to have died from
her treacherous caresses. The strangest thing about her was the
way she could act at a distance. My father's continual trips all
over town on his bicycle were a kind of allegory of Electricity's
invisible flight to the farthest corners, and the most intimate
… But if you think about it, everything is allegory. One thing
signifies another, even the fact that I have ended up becoming a
writer and composing this true account. To follow the prompts
of allegory, which also works by remote control, I too could be
practicing a trade for which I am quite unqualified, manipulat-
ing objects—memories, for example—of which I know and
understand nothing, in a state of utter puzzlement. But that
doesn't alter the reality of the facts: my father was an electrician
and I am a writer. These are real allegories.

The problem for my father was that after 1955 the march
of History began, and he was left behind. Everyone remembered the good old days. What else could they do? Those good

old days were all they had. But while they were remembering, things continued to happen, and next time they looked, everything had changed. Life grew richer; novelties came to Pringles; the twentieth century finally arrived. Science spilled its horn of plenty over that far-flung corner of the nation, nourishing the snobbery of the barbarians. It all seemed like make-believe, as frivolous and insubstantial as a topic of idle conversation, and yet, as in a magic trick, it became reality.

I absorbed everything. My curiosity had no limits; it was as if an intellectual spell had broken the frames that normally structure a child's education. Modernity poured into me like a wild torrent, and I mixed everything up.

Opposite our house was an accountant's office where I would go when I had nothing else to do; I ran errands for the accountant and his clerk (who was his nephew). Since the clerk was often absent, the accountant used to leave me to look after the office when he went out. My sole function was to be there and, if anyone came, to say that the accountant had gone out and would be back soon. The clientele consisted of small farmers, for whom the accountant "did the books." Their visits to town were rare; they usually had plenty of time on their hands, and a need to talk that had been building up in the solitude of the plains. I listened to those endless conversations with an inexhaustible avidity. They always seemed too short; I wanted more. Later, on my own, I reproduced them mentally, and even enriched them, giving them a new dimension of endlessness.

That was how I heard about the accelerating pace of change.

Novelty glowed like a will-o'-the-wisp. My sources were country folk, uneducated and prone to lying, but that only made the whirlwind of History seem more marvelous. For example, there was talk of the new hybrids. Wheat could produce grains the size of chickpeas; the increase in take (as they called the yield colloquially) was amazing. Summer after summer, I followed the rise of the yields as if I had invested in them, calculating each farmer's earnings. A yield of ten sacks per hectare would cover the costs; seventy sacks would make the lucky harvester rich. And now, suddenly, they were talking about seventy sacks as an absolute minimum; soon a single grain would be big enough to fill a sack. And the density of the product was increasing exponentially. Curiously, the number of sacks never exceeded seventy, I don't know why, but there were other figures to take into account. I did the calculations mentally, memorized the results, then looked up the Chicago grain prices in *La Nueva Provincia*, did the multiplications, and was staggered by the gigantic results. All these castles in the air were demolished by the curious fact that the hybrid grains were utterly useless. That wheat was no good for making flour, or anything else. The increase in size and density was achieved at the cost of utility. So what was it all about? It seemed like an enormous sham. But of course I must have been getting it all wrong. My knowledge was derived from idle or mendacious chatter, and I couldn't fit what I had heard into any kind of system; bits of information that had dropped haphazardly from bragging or hypocritical lips piled up haphazardly on the warped shelves of my fantasy.

The farmers were always lying; and when they didn't lie, they exaggerated. They lied about themselves, and exaggerated about everyone else. One of their favorite pretexts for exaggeration was the extension of the electrical grid into rural areas. They were always telling stories about going back to their candlelit farmhouses at night and seeing, far off in the pitch-black country darkness, some recently electrified ranch house. The Asteinza place, the Iturrioz place, the Domínguez place ... Each time it was somewhere new, a dazzling sun in the middle of the night: houses, sheds, gardens, even the stockyards ... "Unbelievable! So beautiful! That's progress!" If you could believe what they said, the woodlands were festooned with lights; the eucalyptuses had become Christmas trees.

There was a typewriter in the office. Since I spent many hours there alone, I was naturally tempted to give it a try. And I yielded repeatedly to that temptation. At first I did it in secret, then one day the accountant caught me at it and didn't tell me off, so I went on doing it when he was there. I spent whole afternoons at the typewriter. I don't know what I wrote: whatever. Once I asked the accountant: "Should you leave a space after a comma?" He thought about it. Then he bent over my shoulder to look, saw my comma, and noticed something else:

"Look! You don't put a comma before *and*—never."

That wasn't what I'd asked, although he did have a point because I had put a comma before *and*. I hated it when things got mixed up; even at that age I had an organized mind, and I liked to keep everything clear and under control. This sequence of a comma and the word *and* was accidental. I tried to show that I was grateful for the tip, but returned to my initial question. He nodded and said he wasn't sure; he'd never really focused on that detail. But there was a way to check. On a shelf, among the dossiers, he had an encyclopedia of accounting in three volumes. I remember those volumes well, because they were the first books I ever held; and although I often handled and even read them (without understanding a thing), I too had overlooked that detail, which the practice of writing had just brought to my notice.

He opened one of the volumes and looked … It was a random page from a volume chosen at random (each had about a thousand pages); he adjusted his gaze to the spatial relations of the written universe, and finally focused …

"Well, how about that? Here's a comma right before *and* …"

Perhaps it was the only case in which the writers of the encyclopedia had departed from the rule, and he had chanced upon it. (In the previous sentence I have put a comma before *and*, correctly I believe, which goes to show that this "rule" is pretty shaky.)

That's as much as I remember. But the rest is easy enough to reconstruct: we must have come to the conclusion that a space should be left after a comma, as after any other punctuation mark.

My friend Osvaldo Lamborghini once told me that he too, when learning to type as a boy, had discovered the space that follows punctuation marks. It seems to be something that you

have to discover: it's not taught at school, nor is it spontane-
ously perceived in the act of reading. For Osvaldo, it was decisive. Telling me about it, decades later, he was still moved by
the memory, and he fixed me with those dark, oriental eyes
of his, gazing through the cigarette smoke, to make sure that I
had understood: that space, so subtle and refined, had won his
undying loyalty. It showed him that writing, as well as having
a communicative function, could also convey an elegance, and
that, he realized, was where his destiny lay. He was always very
sensitive to such things. A mutual friend used to say, "Osvaldo
doesn't have a style so much as a way of punctuating." Which
is why, ten years after his death, I wrote a little novel about the
comma, in homage to him.

I have strayed from my theme, but not too far. One never really strays beyond the possibility of return. On one occasion,
the big window right across the front of the accountant's office was covered with a kind of white paint, which was used
back then to stop people looking into stores and businesses.
I seem to remember that this substance was known as "liquid
chalk." How odd. I don't know why it fell out of use, but then
I'm not really sure why it was necessary either, or why it had
been used on that particular occasion. Although I do remember clearly what it was like. It was applied with a brush to the
inside surface of the glass, covering it with a perfectly smooth,
white film. And you could write perfect letters on the chalked
window with a fingertip; indeed the owners of the stores ex-
ploited this possibility to leave messages for their clients, such

as: "Reopening soon," or "Under new ownership," or any other practical information that justified the infantile pleasure of writing on such an inviting surface. For children, the temptation was irresistible. Kids from the neighborhood used to visit when I was "on duty," and naturally we couldn't resist: we ended up covering the window with inscriptions. But there's a trick to that writing: for it to be legible from outside, you have to write in reverse, back to front. The only way to do it is to use capitals, thinking carefully before you draw each letter, with a kind of double vision or ad hoc mental adjustment, and even so, you're bound to end up with an *R* or an *S* the wrong way around. When the inscriptions consisted of more than one word, I noticed the importance of the space, which like so many other things took on real significance when considered in reverse. Later I discovered that in the early days of writing, in Greco-Roman antiquity, the space between letters didn't exist. And it strikes me now, on reflection, that the invention of the space may have been as fundamentally important as the invention of zero in mathematics, and that the two may have been closely related.

I remember this banal episode of naughtiness because it was the only time the accountant got really cross with me, and even threatened to banish me from his office. In general, he was very tolerant, partly because of his character, partly because I was well behaved, and partly too no doubt because I was useful, and he must have felt guilty about exploiting me without any kind of recompense. On this occasion, though, he bawled me out:

"Did you think I wouldn't notice? ... Writing all this without permission is bad enough ... But prohibited words!" That was when I began to realize what it was about. It wasn't simply the fact that we had written on the glass and spoiled its whiteness, but the specific words that we had put there; not the form, but the content. I hadn't really thought about that. Absorbed by the challenge of writing backwards, I hadn't stopped to consider the meanings, and now I understood: caught up in the excitement, the rush and the recklessness of the crime, we could have written all kinds of horrors. It wasn't myself I was worried about— even my reflexes were sensible and repressed—but my friends, who were little savages. "They've written F U C K for sure," I thought, and hung my head. The accountant fumed a bit longer and then forgot about it. And that was the end of the incident.

But the epilogue was still to come, a few hours later that afternoon (one of those interminable summer afternoons in Pringles). I was on my own in the office, waiting for the accountant to return; it was after his normal closing time. I was sitting on the high bench with my elbows resting on the counter and my fists pressed into my cheeks. My mind was a blank. I had succumbed to the vague, unmotivated melancholy of childhood, accentuated by the time of day and no doubt also by the fact that I was facing a window painted white, like a wall. Without being able to see the sky, I could sense that it was turning a phosphorescent pink. That's what happens in the last hour of those glorious summer evenings in Pringles: the air is illuminated; its corpuscles shimmer. And then a word appeared, in fat, pink letters on the dark wood of the counter, right in front of me, just where it would have been if I had written it: PERÓN. Hallucinatory, spellbinding, and real as could be, although it seemed impossible. I recoiled, blinking wildly. It was still there, written with a paintbrush dipped in light. Eventually I looked up and saw that the light on the counter was projected through one of the scribbles in the painting on the window. That was the prohibited word the accountant had been talking about. I was so inattentive I never would have noticed it among all the doodles and inscriptions covering the lower half of the whited glass. The sky had to reveal it to me, like a new MENE MENE TEKEL UPHARSIN. A further source of amazement was awaiting me when the surprise receded and I recovered my powers of reason: the word was projected the right way around and not in reverse.

There is a game called "little mirrors" ... I've just discovered this here in Rosario, where I have come to spend a few days, while continuing to record these memories (because I keep writing wherever I am and whatever else is happening). The name is apt: I knew the game, but not the name, and now, for me, the two will always go together. I knew the game as a boy, and it was a girl who named it for me just now, which has set me wondering about the continuity of childhood. I would be the first to agree that nothing is eternal, but I have to admit that there is a kind of thought that runs underneath History, though no one can say who passes it on. Children don't have instruments for transmitting thought from one generation to another, so they must keep reinventing it. In this case the continuity spans half a century and the distance from Pringles to Rosario; it reaches back to another world, another time ... Present circumstances are providing ample opportunity to observe and investigate this phenomenon, since the real purpose of my trip (the excuse was a conference on the Rhetoric of the Essay) was to meet and catch up with a number of children. It so happens that among my friends in Rosario, who are all fanatical literary theorists, having children has come into fashion. The days spent here have been most instructive. Last night I went to dinner at Adriana's place; she was the first to reproduce, when I was just getting to know the group. My first trip to Rosario coincided with the birth of her daughter Cecilia, whose growth I followed up to the age of three or four but no farther. So last night was a surprise. When I went up onto the terrace of their house on Calle España, a great big girl, almost as tall as me, was tracing vertiginous circles on roller skates. She came over to give me a kiss, with a radiant smile. "Cecilia! You're so tall! And so pretty!" I wasn't just being polite. That tall (almost towering) ten-year-old girl, flushed from the exercise, with her bright eyes, was literally glowing. She was off again straight away to continue her loops in the moonlight, striking sparks from the red tiles, and she would have gone on all night if her father hadn't yelled at her. Later, during the meal, Cecilia mentioned the "little mirrors." They are ways of turning an insult around to return it to the sender. But the one she mentioned was very basic: "For you and all your family." I seized the opportunity to enrich it: "In Pringles, we used to say it with a rhyme, Cecilia: 'For your relatives in all the zoos, and especially for you.' It sounds better that way, and it's more effective." She wasn't convinced. With a child's implacable logic, she judged the rhyme to be defective: "Shouldn't you say 'yous'?" I was about to tell her that it was the other way around: you should say "zoo," because working-class children in Pringles used to drop the *s*; but I kept quiet, because I felt that my intellectual hosts here in Rosario might not appreciate that clarification. I remembered other "little mirrors," but kept them to myself because they were not suitable for polite company. There was a very concise and definitive one that was used to answer the traditional "your mother" insults: "Filthy swine! Yours, not mine!" The proverbial brevity of the comeback encapsulates something true. A woman, whatever the insult says about her, has her children one after another, and the turn of that little phrase neatly renders the impossibility of one and the same woman having given birth to both adversaries. Of course a woman can have many children over the years, but I should remind the reader that we were all only children, and each of us had only one mother.

There was another "little mirror" that was much more direct. In fact it was a counter-mirror. It was used when the insult was: "Your mother's twat." The "mirror" went: "You mean your sister's, I saw you kissed hers." And then the first kid could come back with the definitive retort: "When it came to sisters, my parents passed, so I'm gonna have to make do with your ass." Indeed, none of us had sisters, which is why for many years I assumed that those rhymes were specific to Pringles.

Of the conversations that I heard in the accountant's office, it was the monologues that I found most inspiring. And oddly (or maybe it's not so odd, given my taciturn nature), this preference for monologue over dialogue has continued. I think it is related to my morbid fascination with madness, particularly the madness that is latent in normality, one step away from the most secure and comforting daily routine, as opposed to the sort that is confined to mental asylums. In monologues people "give themselves away." But there was something more: as I listened I could follow the slow and magnificent growth of imaginary constructions, in which language, spinning freely in a void, eventually opened onto something beyond words.

Back then, people had so much time, they would tolerate the craziest monologues. I can't have been the only one who listened to them with pleasure. The tenant farmers who visited the office were always sounding off. The accountant could hold his own too; in fact, he was the worst. And he repeated himself with his various interlocutors. No one else was privy to the repetition, and this I found inexpressibly satisfying. I noted the variations, the expansions, the refinements, and later, on my own, I went over the stories again, adding and varying and polishing even more. One of his (and my) favorites was about a tramp's "accounts." These, of course, were tax returns, which the accountant had attended to in his professional capacity. The tramp in question, a staple character, was one of those vagabonds from the fringes of Buenos Aires who were numerous at the time. The story was that he had once gone to complain to the Revenue Service inspectors. Like all Argentinian citizens, he was supposed to pay taxes. There were plenty who didn't, of course, but the charm of this story lay in the fact that the tramp had no need to lie, because he conducted his life entirely outside the system of monetary exchange. This is where the accountant launched into his expansions, becoming a keeper of narrative accounts, a recounter (and there, incidentally, he was on firmer ground, because in the field of financial account-keeping, he was self-taught and had no formal qualifications at all). He would switch back and forth between the roles of the increasingly perplexed tax inspectors and the tramp, who had an answer for everything. "House or apartment?" "No." "Ah, so you rent?" "No, I sleep under the bridge." "Dependants?" "Just me." "Clothing?" "I make do with my old threads." "And what if they wear out or tear?" "People give me stuff. No, actually, I use old sacks." And so it went. "Food?" This was the most colorful category. His favorite seasonal dish: watercress from the river. What he represented, fundamentally, was the utopic state of nature, but the story didn't make me long for the past, because I sensed how anachronistic this character was, and although I planned to be like him one day (what little boy could resist that dream?), I wanted to do it in the modern world where taxes are paid and people are part of big, efficient social machines.

Dimly aware that modernity was threatening my father, I thought of it as an individual journey into the future: you would wake up in the morning to discover that a hundred years had passed and everything was different. A certain imaginative refinement led me to scorn spaceships and skyscrapers covered with glass. The change would be a matter of style: something invisible yet decisive. For example, a man from the time before the invention of zero, who has magically traveled to the time after, walking down the street and looking around . . . Or the same thing, but with the space between written words. Or, and this is more subtle, a man from the time in which the word "Perón" was prohibited, transported to a time in which that prohibition has been lifted. In writing this account, I am performing something like that leap in time: not between styles, because my style hasn't changed since I was a child, but between effects of style. Except that I'm doing it in reverse, from the future to the past; and yet by virtue of writing and the transparency of style the reverse becomes the right side, that is, the reverse of the reverse.

Occasionally the men who came to the office were somewhat more enlightened and reasonable. They were the exceptions. Instead of launching into crazy monologues, they provided an opportunity to hear some truth, and although what they said gave me none of the pleasure that I got from fiction, it was their point of view that I adopted, albeit reluctantly. It was as if, in spite of my inclinations and tastes, I was destined to belong to that other world, the arid world of reason. On one occasion, such a man, who was strangely well informed about my family and its peculiarities, began to explain what life held in store for the children of the town. "Nobody wants to be a worker anymore," he said. "Nobody wants to work!" agreed his interlocutors enthusiastically, assenting to one of those pessimistic generalizations that are never all that general, because they always fail to include the person who proffers them. But this man had a more precise idea to convey; he wasn't just indulging in cut-rate demagogy. "No one wants to get their hands dirty practicing a trade. I don't know if it's because they're ashamed of manual work, or if they're just being overoptimistic, but parents aren't doing their children any favors by sending them to study at those secretarial academies like the one Velásquez runs, instead of teaching them their own trades. They think that if their son goes to work in a coat and tie he'll be more important than the guy in overalls, but in fact he'll end up as a two-bit office worker without a future." The others, who had always been too busy talking to get around to thinking, grumpily agreed. The man turned to me, and to my surprise (showing that he really did know more than he'd been letting on) said:

"You're Linden Tree's son, aren't you?"

"Yes."

"A case in point. An electrician: he could easily teach his son the trade. With the demand there is for electricians, and it's only going to increase. But no, these people's idea of progress is to put their son behind a desk, so he can molder for the rest of his life on a miserable salary."

Et cetera. His diagnosis was diabolically accurate. Which is not to say that he was right to criticize "these people" for their naive desire to climb the social ladder that seemed to be at their disposal. After all, only the "other" people could reason like this, people like him: the ones who had kicked Perón out and started the cruel march of History. And yet what he was saying was true. All the boys I knew, without exception, once they finished primary school, went to the Velásquez Academy, and then entered the world of business and bureaucracy. It was a dream, a hope, an evolutionary goal.

With his penetrating comments and criticism, this man was placing himself on a superior level. From there, he could offer an accurate diagnosis, but he couldn't understand. On the level where things were happening, it all looked different. There, the Velásquez Academy was the reasonable option, answering real needs. The full course of studies was barely two years long, and as soon as the student graduated, at the age of fourteen, he or she was ready to enter the labor market, which seemed to have an insatiable need for young accounting clerks.

The irrational option, on the other hand (from the point of view of the people actually involved), was the very prestigious National College. There it would take no less than five years to attain the secondary education certificate, which was absolutely useless when it came to finding a job; the only thing it was good for was entry to a university, and the universities were in Buenos Aires and La Plata, far away and inaccessible. So unless you were rich, to send your child to the National College was absurdly aspirational, or simply a waste of time.

The worst thing, according to the neighborhood commentators, was that the college adhered to the official syllabus, determined by esoteric objectives so remote from practical needs that they became a source of jokes. For example, one of the subjects studied in first year (which is as far as the investigations had gone) was Botany. And what possible use could Botany be to the offspring of a humble family whose first and urgent concerns would be to help his parents financially, to carve out a future, and arm himself effectively for the struggle to survive. Botany, truly! In the neighborhood, the discipline came under savage attack, perhaps because of its sonorous name. There must have been, and surely were, more useless subjects, but Botany was the paradigmatic example.

I lied knowingly when I said that there were no exceptions to the "Velásquez project." There was one; it was flagrant and notorious, and, for a season, it brought the word Botany back onto everyone's lips. This was a boy who lived on my block, the only son (naturally) of the poorest family in the neighborhood. They weren't just poor: the father didn't work; he spent all day smoking in the doorway. No one knew how they survived; relatives must have been helping them out. The mother was a thin Indian lady dressed in black, always shut up in the kitchen. The boy was three years older than me, so he was finishing sixth grade when I was about to go into fourth. And then, to the infinite surprise of the whole neighborhood, they sent him to the College! It was so ridiculous it beggared imagination. And yet, in a way, it was predictable.

This boy—I'll call him M—was involved in an episode that I remember well. One day, one afternoon, my mother and I went out, heading for the center of town, I can't remember why. The center was exactly five blocks away, but we never went there, so this was a momentous excursion. We set off, and M, who was hanging around in the street, tagged along. This was during his time at the College—a short time, incidentally, two or three months, no more, because his parents had an attack of sanity: they changed their minds and sent him to the Velásquez Academy, a decision that was announced in the neighborhood with a good deal of vindictive smirking. The three of us set off walking very happily down the middle of the street. M was a pleasant, talkative, uninhibited boy. My mother had dressed up for an "outing," and that was why we were walking in the middle of the street: her formal attire included shoes with towering stiletto heels. Unused to wearing them, she was tottering along as if on stilts, and the smooth asphalt of the road was much safer for her than the stones and weeds of the unsealed sidewalk.

My mother was very short, almost a dwarf. Or rather, she had the stature of a dwarf, along with other physical characteristics that were as unusual and conspicuous as those of dwarfism, but different. For example, her head was strikingly small (or perhaps it was in proportion to her body, but since she was so short, the "normal" thing would have been a dwarf's big head). It was covered with a gray down instead of hair, which never grew long enough to be combed or brushed (luckily it was too fine to bristle). The most arresting thing about her, though, were the glasses: small and round, and so exceptionally thick that they looked for all the world like marbles. They had been made for her when she was four years old, and she had been wearing them ever since. In spite of her shortness, and her rather grotesque appearance, she had an air of authority and stateliness that imposed respect. Everyone called her madam, which was unusual, because we called the other mothers in the neighborhood by their first names, or even their nicknames.

Anyway, as we reached the corner, a car swerved to overtake us, and since another car was audible in the distance, Mom reconsidered and came to the conclusion that we could stay on the asphalt without having to walk right in the middle of the street.

She said: "We're going to walk nearer to the curb; we don't want some bumbling driver to run us over."

M looked at her in astonishment, and asked at the top of his voice (that was how he always spoke): "Bumbling? What does that mean?"

"Don't you know what bumbling means? Clumsy."

M burst into happy, exuberant laughter: "No! That can't be right! It's not a real word; you just made it up!"

My mother smiled, very pleased with herself. M's suspicion was not unreasonable; it was just the kind of thing she liked to do: inventing mysterious words, concocting enigmas, playing jokes. On this occasion, she merely clicked her tongue, delighted with the mystification.

M insisted: "It's not a real word! It's not in the dictionary!"

I was stunned by this. "It's not in the dictionary." It would be hard to convey the impact of that sentence. First, I should point out that all the aspersions cast on the College had gradually turned it into a myth, something vague and obscure, and therefore irresistibly attractive. Botany itself, although (or perhaps because) I didn't know what it was, had become mythical in my mind. All that useless knowledge, which being useless had no limits and could cover or duplicate the whole world, or rather the worlds (both visible and invisible), was a vortex, a magnet. But M's sentence transported me to a higher level. "It's not in the dictionary" implied that M knew how many and which words *were* in the dictionary. Knew them all, since he was convinced that one in particular wasn't there. A random word, taken from a lady's lexical flourish in the course of a casual conversation, and he could instantly place it in the gap, the void, left by the totality of existing words. I had never opened a dictionary (the only book that I had handled was the Encyclopedia of Accounting), but I knew what it was. A dictionary contained all the words, and with all the words, in various combinations, all the other books were made. M was the only boy I knew who had gone to the College. The conclusion of the syllogism was that at the college they learned the dictionary. I felt at once affirmed and released. What would have been an almost sadistic punishment for any normally constituted boy (studying the dictionary) was what I had been born to do. Encyclopedism and combinatorics were my domain, and it was a domain that went on growing, like a dawn.

The well-founded suspicion that my friend was wrong on this occasion did not in any way affect the thrilling certitude that I felt: the mistake was an accident; it could be corrected. M, like the rest of my friends, could never resist a crude joke, and he may well have supposed that my mother was trying to crack one, in her lame way, by using the invented word "bumbling" to mean "bumping into somebody's bum." (Here I should add, to be fair, that M is now a wealthy rancher, a millionaire. And not because he studied at the College, where he only spent a few months, but thanks to the accounting skills that he learned at the Velásquez Academy.)

I too was destined for the College. This had been decided long before, by my mother. The decision was firm, as if decreed by fate, like everything that she controlled. My mother announced it with the haughty, classist confidence that was part and parcel of her irrationality. When the family had sacrificed itself for five exhausting years, and I finally had my certificate, which university would I attend? The odd thing was that my father, although himself quite capable of reasoning, silently supported her. Perhaps it was a form of suicide, some kind of suicide pact between them ...

It has been said that every marriage is a suicide pact. It might be true, in a metaphorical and poetic sense, but adjustments would have to be made for the historical circumstances in each particular case. To understand a single metaphor you sometimes have to go back through the causes, and the causes of the causes. In the case of my parents, the pact could only have been

figurative, so great was the difference between their psycho-
logical styles. There was no common level where they could
meet to agree on objectives and conditions. They were living
in separate worlds, different dimensions, which were mutually
irreducible or even inconceivable. But it would be a mistake to
presume that this is what made me so strange because it's something that every child has to go through. Which sounds like an
exaggeration: if it were really true, someone might object, we
would all be condemned to schizophrenia, and society would
be threatened with imminent self-dissolution. I could stand
firm in the face of that objection. I could say: Yes, so what?
But no, it's not like that, I admit. Instead of dissolution, there
is History. The tearing apart is worked out over time. But here
is where I dig in my heels: it doesn't work out well; there is no
happy ending. Didn't Ortega y Gasset say, with all the authority of a philosopher and a Spaniard, that "humanity is divided
into idiots and monsters," presuming that there was no third
possibility? The best we can hope for is to become monsters,
although it means renouncing happiness.

I should attempt a description of the point where the hetero-
geneous dimensions came together, the magical, inconceivable
place where things destined never to meet entered into contact.
The house, the neighborhood, the town … I'll begin with the
house where we lived. It was the ruins of an old inn, which in
the glory days of Pringles must have served as a kind of hotel.
Back then, it seems, buildings were amply proportioned, and
constructed solidly enough to withstand decades of neglect

and abuse. This one traced a majestic L, facing onto intersecting streets. In the corner, and along one of the streets, there
were big sitting rooms, kitchens, store rooms, and what must
have been the staff quarters. The entrance, which was very
grand, was on that side, and where the building came to an
end there was a gateway, once used by carriages and cars. The
guest rooms, about ten of them, were all in a row on the other
side, with barred windows onto the street, and doors opening
onto a gallery with iron columns. A garden with old trees took
up the rest of the property, which covered half a block. We occupied one of the guest rooms, just one. The rest of the building was empty and dilapidated. Moldings, scrolls, and false columns abounded. On the corner, over the majestic front door
that opened onto the main sitting room, there was still a stucco
coat of arms. The establishment was probably designed for rural clients who might not have felt at home in the other hotels
that must have already existed in the center of Pringles. Because of its peripheral location, five hundred yards out, it was
almost in the country; and with its vast grounds (the whole
block originally), it would have been better suited to the ac-
commodation of carriages and horses than the more centrally
located alternatives. With the growth of the town, in the second and third decades of the century, the need for such an inn
vanished; it closed down, and its shell remained there, embed-
ded in the neighborhood. Its owners had been French, part of
a large community in the region. A significant fact revealed the
building's antiquity: there was not, and there had never been,

a single bathroom. There was a latrine at the bottom of the garden, built in the same palatial style as the rest.

As I said, the three of us were the only inhabitants of that enormous building. But we occupied only one of its rooms, which was our whole home: kitchen, dining room, living room, and bedroom all in one. I didn't find it poor or uncomfortable; I had always lived like that, and all the families that I knew, that is, the families of my friends in the neighborhood, made do with similar spaces, all of them smaller than ours. It's important to remember that these were all one-child families, so the conditions were not wretched, as they would have been with eight children or ten, or an indefinite and constantly growing number. Our setup was really a kind of adaptation. Far from finding it unfortunate, I considered this use of a single space to be the simplest and most reasonable system. Anything else would have seemed extravagant, as it would seem to a child today to have different dining rooms for soup and dessert, or a bedroom for the siesta and another for the night. Despite their more varied experience, my parents must have felt as I did, because it never occurred to them to colonize one of the many empty rooms all around us.

Even so, this limitation might have been overdetermined by the conditions, or rather the history, of the lease. I never learned how my parents ended up in that building or why they were the only ones who did. But it wasn't hard to work out. At some point during the Peronist decade rents were frozen, which was a boon to tenants, given the subsequent rates of inflation. And the

Revolución Libertadora, which changed so many other things, could not change that. There was no incentive for the owners of that old ruin, descendants of the French migrants who had built it, to put in new tenants. We must have been an experiment, and it didn't turn out well. Also, the building was the object of difficult probate proceedings. Once a year, they hung a red flag at the corner and put up a sign announcing the judicial sale. When the day came, an auctioneer turned up, and a little ceremony was organized on the sidewalk: it was very brief and always the same. An audience of regulars gathered, all of them men; my father never missed it, nor did I. The owners came too; I don't know how they were related—brothers or cousins or brothers-in-law—in any case, they hated each other with a passion. The two parties never communicated and kept their distance. The auctioneer gave a little speech that he had prepared in advance: the measurements of the property, indoor area, party walls, etc. Then he would announce the reserve price, lift his hammer, wait a few seconds in silence, or murmuring something, and close the proceedings. Precisely at that moment, the owners would walk off in opposite directions without saying a word, looking serious and sad. Using the hood of a car as a desk, a notary who had come with the auctioneer would fill out a form, sign it, and ask two witnesses, usually neighbors, to sign as well.

Thanks to my father's explanations, I finally came to understand the meaning of this curious negative ceremony, which was repeated every year throughout my childhood. I have already mentioned that no women attended. My mother didn't come with us, but there was something deliberate and defiant about her absence. During the days that followed the auction, she would be irritable, combative, and grumpy, although she was normally as cheerful and carefree as a songbird. My father tried over and again to explain the meaning of what had taken place, but she didn't understand, and his volatile impatience ended up setting off furious arguments. Her bewilderment seemed quite irrational to me, because in the end even I had come to grasp the workings of that performance (just describing them used up all my father's meager store of calm). The magistrate in charge of the probate proceedings would order that the property be auctioned. But for the auction to be carried out, there had to be a buyer. If no one bid, all the related cases had to be reopened, in turn, until this one came up again. It was that simple. Why couldn't my mother accept it? Why did she have to complicate things with irrelevant questions, complaints, and sniping? This was the only situation in which she departed from the policy of hosing down her explosive husband.

The key point in the disagreement, the thing that my mother refused to understand, was that none of the owners ever seized the opportunity to buy the others out and put an end to the farce. And yet the reason was perfectly clear. Since there were no bids, there was no sale, and both parties went on being owners without having spent a peso. Had there been a bid, the mutually hostile branches of the family would have kept raising it ... It would have set off an endless bidding war, because both sides were determined to have it all for themselves. The danger was always there. Not that either side would have lit the fuse, but someone else might have come along, someone without any connection to the family and unaware of the feud, who might have had the rash idea of buying the place to knock it down and build a new house. This was an issue for us especially, since we were the ones who lived there. A curious consequence of the feud was that back in the early days, before I was born, when my father went to pay the rent, the owners said that they couldn't give him a receipt. That document, I suppose, would have altered the legal status of the arrangement. My father replied that if they weren't giving him a receipt, he wasn't going to pay. It was a stalemate, and from that point on, he never paid again. In other words, as well as having fixed rent, we didn't pay it.

All my friends lived in miserable, cramped little houses. We had plenty of space, but with the proud dignity of the poor we scorned it and went on living within the same four walls. We didn't even use more of the gallery than the part directly in front of our room. I was forbidden to go into the other rooms, although most of them had no door and were visited only by rats. Not that I was all that tempted. Sometimes, when my parents were out, the neighborhood kids would come and explore, but that was very rare. I was also forbidden to play in the garden, or even to stray from the paths that led to the latrine and the pump (we didn't have running water either), and I internalized this prohibition so thoroughly that there were corners where I never set foot.

Nonetheless, the building had an ⟨
shaping my imagination. Ever since th⟨
the form of a palace. To get to sleep⟨
ited all those empty rooms ... Or n⟨
didn't know how many there were; I r⟨
of counting them. I lost myself in tha⟨
was sleep. It might not seem like mu⟨
tion on, and with it the course of a whole life. But apart from
the fact that small causes have been known to produce large effects, the cause is not so small in this case, because the circumstances dissolved the contradiction between Palace and Room,
and launched a mechanism for dissolving all contradictions.

I never knew (and since I never knew that I didn't know,
I didn't ask) why we lived in that room and not in one of the
others. There were so many, and they were all the same ... Although, of course, they weren't really the same; each had its
own location, and that made an irreducible difference. The
only distinguishing feature of our room, except for the obvious fact that it had been kept in a state that was fit for human
habitation, was a fireplace. A big, marble fireplace. None of the
other rooms had one. Who knows what forgotten function that
room may have originally fulfilled. One day, in the course of
my reading I came across the expression "the Winter Palace,"
which set me dreaming; I thought I could alter it to reflect my
personal experience. I would make it "the Winter Room in the
Palace of the Seasons."

Once, in the midst of the ceaseless chatter that my mother

p to calm my father's nerves, she said that when they had come to live there, as newlyweds, they had used the fireplace for cooking, over a wood fire, as in the Middle Ages. This excited me; it appealed to my childish belief in the superiority of olden times. I would have liked to see it. I asked her to make a meal that way, just one; but she didn't humor me. She said that when I grew up I could ignore progress and return to the Middle Ages as often as I liked. Apparently that phase of their life had been very brief; as soon as my father received his first pay packet as council electrician, he bought his wife an enormous Volcán kerosene stove, which we still had. It had stayed in the place where the delivery men had put it, against one of the internal walls, right in the middle. The room was square, and each wall had a central marker of some kind: on the gallery side, the door; opposite that, on the street side, the window; the Volcán stove on one internal wall; and on the other, the old fireplace. That symmetry delighted me; I kept finding new meanings in it. The floor was wooden, made of narrow boards, and sounded hollow. The biggest piece of furniture was the double bed, against the internal wall beside the fireplace, on the door side. On the window side, my bed and a big closet. In front of my bed, beside the stove, a very tall and spacious wardrobe with three mirrors. Finally, the table and chairs, in the corner on the door side. This arrangement never changed.

It was our little world, our refuge and our secret. Or at least in retrospect it seems there must have been a secret, to justify the arrangement, if only as a mnemonic device. The strange thing is, there wasn't, and yet I remember it all perfectly. We weren't cramped. I was out in the street all day, Dad too, because of his work, and Mom was a real "door lady": she would take a chair out onto the sidewalk, and sit there knitting all afternoon. She used to say that she had started doing it when I began to walk, to keep an eye on me, and then it became a habit. People passing by must have thought, "What a big house that lady has," not realizing that the real house was hidden in the heart of the house they could see, as a seed lies hidden within a forest.

Inside the room, there was another outside: the radio. We kept it on the table, sitting on a stand, and it was always on if there was anyone at home. We listened to music, news, comedy programs, and quizzes. Mom followed the soap operas, and so did I, the ones about gauchos, written by Chiappe. For Mom it was proof of my filial and familial devotion that I would always interrupt my games and adventures to sit down with her and listen to Juan Carlos Chiappe's radio plays. She mentioned this proudly to the ladies in the neighborhood. But I didn't do it out of loyalty; I did it for pleasure.

It was also via the radio that politics entered our home. I would have led a less tortured life if that subject had been kept out, as it should have been, for many reasons, the chief of which is that it led to disillusion. It has often been said, with good reason, that Peronism was not a genuinely popular phenomenon: it came from above, and the people received it as a gift; they went on receiving it until receiving became second nature, and then they began to receive the opposite. This interpretation might seem to be a purely intellectual construction, because in fact the masses felt that they were in control and acted accordingly. And what matters are the facts ("the only truth is reality"); how they came about is secondary. And yet the facts themselves end up justifying the interpretation, because anti-Peronism eventually came from the same direction as Peronism, that is, from above. And when the dream of being able to forge one's destiny evaporated, the result was disillusion, and shame at having been so naive.

My father fell silent, both outwardly and inwardly. This was because he had nothing to say. He internalized the accursed dialectic of History, which penetrated every cell of his cold, dead tongue, and he developed a nervous condition. From then on, he never had enough peace of mind to concern himself with the real life of the nation, which matched or exceeded his own hysteria. Those were years of instability, difficult and chaotic, with frequent changes of government, military rumblings, and interventions. The radio brought us the news. My mother provided the commentary, becoming more voluble as time went by. She had no grasp of politics; she couldn't understand what was going on, and yet she was confident, skeptical, and dogmatic all at once, no doubt emboldened by my father's silence. He must have realized how absurd her comments were and seen how they sprang from astonishing ignorance and childlike arbitrariness, but he kept quiet. And, as the saying goes, silence gives consent.

At some stage, I remember, before an election, the radio kept repeating a slogan: "You choose the government." My mother would snicker sarcastically and reply: "... and Rattenbach chucks them out."

It wouldn't have been so bad (for me, sole witness to this strange war without combatants) if she had confined herself to this embittered cynicism, these occasional ironies. But she began to develop a serious case of visceral anti-Peronism; her "gorilla" rants became defamatory and truly delirious. This wasn't an ideological development so much as a natural consequence of the decision to talk: talking requires some kind of content. She began to give speeches at mealtimes. She got carried away and couldn't stop. She indoctrinated me. I'd rather not reproduce her words. We all have this sort of confused and paralyzing political background, all of us in Argentina at least. In any case, it didn't last long. The ranting was too absurd to continue, and maybe its function was to provide impetus for the next phase, or to give it structure.

When the subject of politics fell away, speech itself remained. My mother must have discovered that if she spoke, her husband kept quiet, whether she spoke of politics or something else. Being quiet soothed his nerves, or at least tempered their most alarming manifestations. She resorted to her childhood memories, becoming an inexhaustible source of tales, vignettes, scenes, and portraits. In the end I found out about everything. Although she spoke cheerfully of her youth, without airing resentment and even employing a humorous tone, it was one long horror story. She had grown up in the country, the eldest of ten children, who had fallen to her care because of the monstrous indifference of her mother, who was, she said, an example of that exceptional and almost inconceivable figure: the woman devoid of maternal instinct. But the burden that this deficiency had laid on her tender, girlish shoulders compensated for the misfortune of her appearance: her siblings loved her like a mother, rather than regarding her as a goggle-eyed, dwarflike aberration. Her father had died young, and naturally she idealized him.

He died the year she married; I don't know whether it was before or after the wedding, but in that year: forty-eight. That was when her evocations of the past came to an end: she was silent about all that had happened since. She never spoke of her wedding, perhaps because she presumed that we knew all about it (but *I* didn't, and would have been extremely interested to find out). This tact compensated, or overcompensated, for her genuine obsession with marriage in general. Insofar as she saw other people's marriages as eternally given, and was prevented from discussing her own by a powerful taboo, the subject could only be treated, in conversation and thought, via its negation, that is, spinsterhood. She had studied and categorized all the local spinsters; she invented prospects for them, chose "candidates," dreamed up solutions ... But she took infinite pleasure in the failure of these plans, which she saw as a foregone conclusion, and in that she was not mistaken, because all the genuine spinsters I heard about persisted in their condition. It's true

that in her enthusiasm, my mother would sometimes get carried away and apply her favorite label to a girl of twenty (usually a teacher or an office worker), who then promptly went and
got married. But she didn't linger over those exceptions: her
"regular cast" remained unchanged. Not a day went by without
her attending to them. It might seem that she was, unwittingly
and unwillingly, acknowledging the social mobility that Peronism had introduced into Argentinian life, because spinsters
are a specifically middle-class phenomenon, and their appearance in our proletarian milieu could be interpreted as a sign of
upward movement. My mother said as much herself, on occasion: "Those black women always get married, no matter how
ugly they are." And yet the fascination was not incompatible
with her "gorilla" attitude, because the spinsters, by virtue of
the long period required to constitute them as such, predated
Peronism and were still there when it came to an end; the ten
years of the regime had not been enough to produce them, and
that revealed the illusoriness of its aspirations to social change.

There was an image that appeared in the space between my
mother and me, and there it has remained although its origin
was almost divinatory; I deduced it from something she mum-
bled, from an expression or a look. Such minglings of the imagination can occur between mother and son. It was the image of
the fiancées: "the dream of the fiancées …" That's how it has
stayed with me, captured by that formula. My mother, who was
usually so practical, so prosaic and ironic, had once waxed lyri-
cal in describing the bridal gown of a wealthy young woman,

the daughter of a rancher, whose wedding she had attended in her youth: a "dream," a diaphanous white dream of satin, lace, and tulle ... That must have been where the expression came from, but it also corresponded to an objective truth, because all the young girls back then were dreaming of their weddings and their gowns. For them, it was a once-in-a-lifetime chance to be decked out like a princess. It was so absurd ... Yet it was real, it happened; to deny it would have been to deny the evidence of the senses. And the dream took place outside history, unaffected by the vicissitudes of politics and society, as if kept safe in the impregnable casket of a virgin's soul.

My mother had glimpsed something beyond the dream, and somehow I insinuated myself into her gaze ... She had seen the town, Pringles, that is, her whole world, inhabited by fiancées, with their diaphanous white dresses of dream tulle ... All the women were fiancées, all the female inhabitants of that planet, and there were no men, or they weren't part of the vision; the women were all young and beautiful, all "picture perfect," floating in their own personal time (because each would be married "when the time was ripe," when her day came, a day that was unique and exclusively hers, prepared with meticulous attention to detail); there they were in the streets of the town, on its sidewalks, in its patios and houses, seen from above in a bird's-eye view but also through the marveling eyes of a child ... This beautiful utopia was my mother's triumph over time. I complemented it with a fantasy of my own, which strengthened my identification with her. It began with my perverse desire to try on her spectacles, to see the world as she did. I had often asked her if I could, and she had never let me. Since she never took them off, not even to sleep, I hadn't been able to satisfy this whim, but children are stubborn once they get something like this into their heads. I imagined stealing her glasses when she was asleep, plucking them away with a precise movement and running off ... I was always running off, in my fantasies and in reality ... I would put them on when I got out into the street, and then I would see it, if only for an instant (because my mother would be hot on my heels, already rushing out in her nightgown to reclaim her spectacles), that "beautiful utopia," the world of the fiancées ...

About my father's earlier life, I never discovered anything, and I didn't dare to ask. Somehow he had managed to create the impression, among the three of us, that the slightest movement of his thoughts in the direction of the past would trigger an irreversible nervous breakdown. Like those drive mechanisms with a fixed pinion that simply cannot operate in reverse. This must have left its mark on me, because once, many years later, when someone was explaining how the gears of a car worked, I asked, "And what would happen if you were driving in fourth, at a hundred miles an hour, and you put the car into reverse?" This was not a facetious question; I was genuinely curious. Historical circumstances and family responsibilities had clearly oriented my father toward the future; for him, time ran in one direction only. It's logical that he had nothing to say, because the future is made of action, not words.

Only once did he break his silence in a significant way. It was a winter night; I can't remember if it was before or after dinner. There was a radio play on. For my mother this was something serious and cultural, so she had demanded silence; but since she did all the talking, she had to demand it of herself. After a few minutes, I was fed up; I couldn't understand a thing, no doubt because I wasn't trying. I expressed my boredom with snorts and grumbles, which provoked some shushes and a stern glare. I was prone to rebellious outbursts, and had very definite ideas about what was and wasn't fun. Finally, pronouncing my customary, pedantic formula—"I shall retire to my lodgings"—I got up from the table, went and flopped on my bed, and defiantly opened an issue of *Rico Tipo*. I was forbidden to read that magazine—one of many bought by a truck driver who lived nearby, and lent to me by his mother—because of the lewd cartoons, so I usually kept it hidden. But on this occasion I displayed it in a deliberate and noisy way, like a hostile declaration, which I was prepared to back up with arguments: if they were going to force me to listen to some dreary and incomprehensible load of garbage, their prohibitions no longer applied, and I was allowed to do anything to save myself from death by boredom. But the argument I was looking for failed to eventuate, because they didn't look at me or even remember that I was there. I was soon absorbed in the magazine, and my bad mood dissolved; I forgot about them and the radio. I must have read intently for an hour or more; suddenly, the play that they had been listening to was over.

There was a silence. (At some point I must have gone back to the table, because I was involved in the conversation that followed.) Then Mom began to talk again ... but without really launching into a speech: it hadn't crossed her mind that someone else might want to comment first, she was so sure of holding the floor. She was mumbling, still warming up:

"Wonderful! A genius! What talent! García Lorca! ... *Yerma*! He was in Argentina! Margarita Xirgu! ... He was killed in the war!"

That was the way she always talked, without syntax, even when a story carried her away. All the more so in this case, because she had nothing to say. But she could always say something. And her preliminary exclamations conveyed the basic message: what she and her husband had just listened to was real culture, high culture, nothing to do with the Peronists. In fact, that program had unmasked them. The Peronists just had to listen to that play and they would be crushed. It was as if she had said all this, in as many words. She meant it too, and more, much more. She was full of words. It was as if she wanted to take possession of García Lorca's famous play and broadcast it again, herself, for her own benefit ... But she was in no hurry. Half the work was already done. The mere existence of García Lorca was, in itself, a total disaster for Peronism, because he predated the regime, and had outlived it, as that night's program had demonstrated ... He was tangible proof of the trans-Peronist endurance of decent, cultured people, who hadn't been swallowed by the masses ...

Fundamentally, my mother's aspirations were laudable enough. If she didn't express them in a more articulate fashion, it was because she was still dazed by surprise, or plenitude ... Before that play began, she had forgotten all about García Lorca ... But now he was coming back to her, in the voice of her father, who had been a great *zarzuela* fan ... He was coming back along with a flurry of other memories: the popular opera *La del soto del Parral*, the group Los Gavilanes de España, even Tito Schipa ...

And yet, there was something missing. I noticed it myself, not without a vague sense of dread. In spite of her enthusiasm, she was leaving a gap. Everything she was saying or could say related to the outward aspect of the phenomenon: its effect, its prestige, its resonance as a finished object. She wasn't talking about the source of its meaning, that is, the content of the play. Overwhelmed by that heaven-sent opportunity, she probably hadn't registered a single word; her consciousness had been too fully occupied by the opportunity itself to take in its constituent elements.

Which were precisely what my father had something to say about. He had been very thoughtful, deep in concentration. Suddenly he said:

"For a writer to be able to write something like that ..."

This gave Mom such a start!

"What ... ?"

It was true: even a genius had to sit down and write his work.

Things actually had to be done. All the arguments that my mother was preparing, based on praise and satisfaction, were rendered irrelevant by this attack from an unexpected quarter, related to something that turned out to be more primary and basic.

My father, meanwhile, quite unused to argument of any kind, was becoming more and more absorbed in the search for words to capture his fugitive ideas:

"... to write something like that, the opposite of the normal feelings everybody has ... He'd have to ... invent ... or write ... as if he was seeing life ..." He was using gestures to explain himself: his hands were moving over the table. He put his finger on one point, then another, as if indicating nodes of an imaginary diagram, a circuit.

"But what are you ... ? Have you gone ... ?"

"We see life ..." He made a gesture that meant: "from here to out there." "Whereas he ..." Gesture: "from there back to here."

"What ... ? Who ... ?"

"He can't live ... I mean, we can't see ..."

"Maybe *you* can't! ..."

"He's going against the current ... It's as if ..." And here my father found a way to express what he meant, and his voice grew stronger: "It's all in reverse. That's what it is. The writer has to live life in reverse." He went on gesturing, confidently now, as if he could see his idea with perfect clarity, and only had to make me see it. Because he had turned to me and was speaking like a schoolmaster to a pupil. "Everything in life is facing in a certain direction, right? Now imagine it's all turned around the other way . . ."

"Be quiet! Be quiet, will you? Can't you see the boy doesn't understand?"

Then it was as if he had just woken up; he stared at her. He said something unpleasant, like "Idiot . . . fool," I don't know what else, I can't remember. And that was the end of the story. I wasn't deprived of much by Mom's interruption, because it was clear that my father wasn't going to elaborate. Ever since then I've wondered what he meant by "life in reverse." When I read *Yerma* as an adult, I was looking for the key, trying unsuccessfully to reconstruct my father's obscure reasoning.

An anecdote that my mother once told me about her childhood might serve as a model of the strange daily life that History had imposed on us. Any other anecdote would do just as well; some have remained in my memory, others are gone.

The protagonists were two of her younger siblings, a girl and a boy, about seven or eight years old. These two were always fighting, always inventing new reasons to fight, which is not uncommon among siblings. One of the classic themes in this permanent war was command. The boy claimed that the girl was his slave, obliged to do his bidding, without any will of her own. Naturally, as soon as he told her to do something, she would promptly do the opposite, but crafty as he was, he would always come up with some sophistry to affirm that she had in fact obeyed him. For example, he would say, "Shut the window." She would jump up and open it; and he'd come back with "That's what I like: people who do my bidding." "Liar! You told me to shut it, and I opened it!" "But you see I really wanted you to open it, because I'm feeling very hot. If I'd told you to open it, you wouldn't have, would you? But I know you, so I told you to shut it, and I got what I wanted. See how you're always falling into the trap, little slave?" And he would laugh, very pleased with himself. She: "Liar! Bully! I do what I want!" He (dealing the deathblow): "You want proof? The window was shut." That was incontrovertible; and she writhed in impotent rage.

That's how it always played out. He came up with the most ingenious and timely tricks, and in spite of the cruelty behind these machinations, the rest of the family couldn't help admiring his resourcefulness. "It's a pity he doesn't use his intelligence for something more worthwhile!" But they resigned themselves to this behavior, dismissing it as child's play, soon to be outgrown.

And so it was, except that on one occasion, it almost led to disaster. The girl was setting the dining table for the family's lunch. She was doing it to help her mother, but also because she enjoyed the task. Then her brother turned up, on the lookout for opportunities to stir up trouble as usual: "Set the table, I want to eat. Excellent, excellent, that's what I like to see: obedience." This was too crude to hurt, and she barely paid him any attention. Just a disdainful grimace, and she continued with her work as if nothing had happened. She was being very conscientious, carefully placing each item as she had been taught.

Her brother stood there watching and predictably had an idea. He sat down in the chair at the end of the table farthest from the kitchen, the father's place, and adopted a dominant pose, a look of relaxed supremacy, with his little half-closed eyes fixed on her and his head thrown back ... This performance was sufficient in itself to spoil her spontaneity: the awareness of being watched made her movements stiffer and more mechanical. He waited a few seconds, just long enough for her to get into the rhythm, and then he began to give orders, after the fact. She would put a plate in its place, and he would say: "Put that plate down." A fork: "Now put the fork down." A glass: "Now the glass." The girl tried to trick him: she took a plate, went to place it, and as soon as he said, "Put that plate down," she put it back on the pile and set a knife or a napkin on the table. But he carried on unperturbed, accompanying every movement with implacable counter-orders: "No, I changed my mind, better put the knife down first ... Actually, what I want is for you to lay the napkin in its place ..." She would put down a glass: "Put that glass down." She would pick it up and take it back to the sideboard: "Take that glass and put it on the sideboard ... That's what I like: obedience to the master." The poor girl couldn't win. Even if she set out the crockery and cutlery in a sequence of her own choosing, the orders, in spite of following the acts, created an atmosphere of compulsion that surrounded her completely. Her pauses, her changes of pace and direction, and the thousand tricks that she came up with one after another to elude that fate only reinforced the feeling of being a puppet moved by an inescapable power. He savored his triumph, playing with her more and more skillfully; he had plenty of time to slip in self-satisfied remarks: "The slaves are so good these days ... No, that spoon goes on the other side, no, where it was before ... Good! So obedient, these little black slaves we brought from the jungle ..." Sprawled in the chair, with his leg over the arm, he accompanied his orders with the languid gestures of an oriental monarch and smoked an imaginary cigarette to complete the image of the potentate. He exaggerated the rather effeminate grace of his movements in order to heighten the triumphant contrast with his sister's desperate automatism.

"That fork, there ... No, I changed my mind, on the other side ... No, I think I prefer it where it was before ... Better leave it till later ... No, put it down and we're done, there, exactly, thank you, my little servant ..."

But that fork was destined for something else. In a state of extreme frustration, the poor puppet "slave" came up with the one place where her "master" would never tell her to put that implement: she threw it at him. Had she thought it over coolly, she would have come to the conclusion that there was no other course of action left open to her. But she didn't think. She hurled the fork in a blind impulse of fury.

And what happened next made the episode memorable. The fork plunged into the "master's" cheek with such force that it remained there, horizontal and trembling, with its four prongs lodged in the cheekbone, just below the eye. The children's mother, who came when she heard the cries, had to push on the boy's forehead with the heel of one hand and pull on the fork with the other to remove it.

"Half an inch higher and he'd have lost an eye," was the standard reaction, which struck me as banal. It reminded me of that saying about "the master's eye." I preferred to think about the instant before the impact: the fork flying over the table, spinning through the air, like at the circus ... It was a lucky strike, of course. She couldn't have done it again, not even in a thousand tries (I know—I tried). And with a fork, not a knife! Why didn't they do it with forks at the circus?

In any case, that time, there was no retrospective order: victory was hers. And yet, to me, this took nothing away from her brother's earlier victory, which was something I could fully understand and appreciate. At the same time, both of them had failed: the girl, because she had been obliged to abandon the rules of the game; and her brother, because his manipulation of time had come up against the limit of his own body, which stood as an insuperable barrier between the past and the future.

Wasn't that always the way? With Peronism too? And social legislation? "The bonus, all right, make it December." "Now, paid vacations: a union hotel by the beach ... No, in the mountains, that's better. There, perfect." An organized community.

When Peronism became a thing of the past, my mother became a virulent anti-Peronist. I don't think she was the only one. What middle-class Argentina had seen as an "accursed event" affected people who weren't middle class by changing their relation to time. It is time that sets the master-slave dialectic in motion, by inverting it (only an inversion can get it going). That must have been where the idea of "life in reverse" came from. With that expression, I think my father was referring to García Lorca's invention of a barren woman. Why invent a figure like that in life the right way around?

"Life in reverse" is not quite the same as "the world turned upside down." That is something more banal, which I was able to observe on numerous occasions. One example from that time, which left a very clear memory, was an incident that occurred in the house of my friend L, from school. We were inseparable for a time. He was an only child too, but for a reason that made all the difference: his father had died, closing off the possibility of siblings. The rest of us had living fathers who, by contrast, represented calm abstention: they didn't want to have more children; the dead man simply couldn't. The roles were reversed in this fantasy: the dead man was active (had he been alive, he would have gone on procreating), while the living man was passive. And there was an additional difference: L belonged to the middle class. For me, he dwelt in another world. Being fatherless in itself confers a romantic aura, as if life had dealt the child something unthinkable, which since it cannot be thought cannot happen in reality. He lived with his mother in a modern house around the corner from ours; entering it always made me feel slightly dizzy, although at the time I went there every day. It was the only middle-class house I visited in my childhood, and that's why it has stayed with me as an exemplar. From my parents' remarks, and what I can reconstruct now, I know that L and his mother must have been living in fairly straitened circumstances, relying on a modest source of income left by the deceased; but to me they were rich. I didn't need to examine their expenses; it was clear from the house, but most of all from L himself: his character, his style, his nonchalance, his freedom. In the middle of the house was a big sitting room with an enormous table where we did our homework, in the light that flooded in through the French windows opening onto the patio. That constant, overabundant light is the mark of the house in my memory.

L's mother was called Elena, and she spent much of her time at her mother's place, in a faraway part of town. She had two unmarried sisters; perhaps her tragedy had put them off getting married. She was tall, full-bodied, and blonde going prematurely gray. If she was at home, it was because one of the friends with whom she sometimes played canasta had come to visit. Among these ladies was Miss Marta Coco, the music teacher from my school: fat, energetic, friendly, a smoker. I found her fascinating and scary. Luckily she paid me no attention; I don't think she ever spoke to me. She probably didn't even notice my existence. I now know that Miss Marta Coco was a lesbian; back then, she was a lady like any other. She was single, and lived with her mother and a disabled brother.

Once, L and I were sitting at the table doing our homework, and his mother and her friend Marta came and sat down at the other end, carrying what looked like big account books and boxes ... They had brought out their stamp albums. Not theirs, actually, but the albums of their dear departed: Elena's husband and Marta's father. The cult of the dead required them to preserve and enlarge those collections, which had been so important to the deceased. As I was able to infer from their lively chatter, the purpose of this meeting was to look through the albums of Argentinian stamps and swap doubles. They went about it systematically. Both had the Yvert et Tellier catalogs (which Marta complemented with Petrovich's catalog of local stamps), and they manipulated them skillfully. They were concentrating on certain series, laying them out on the table like a game of dominoes or a puzzle, taking stamps from the boxes where they kept the doubles, referring continually to the open albums or the catalogs in order to resolve questions of order, date, value, print quality ... Suddenly I realized that they were looking at the 1952 series showing Evita full-face and in profile, which is very hard to complete because of all the variants: there are forty basic stamps, but for each value there's one printed on local paper and one on imported paper, and the ones on imported paper are either offset printed or photogravure, with an inscription or without (that is, with or without the words EVA PERÓN); there are imperforate pairs, and double prints, and in the brown fifty-cent stamp, a rare error: some were printed on the gum side. There was also the second anniversary stamp, from 1954, with the same design, in three versions. Deep in concentration, with cries of satisfaction when they filled a gap, and of puzzlement when the colors or the perforations didn't match, Elena and Marta relished the pleasures of completion. All collectors strive to complete their collections, no matter what they collect, and in this striving they are aided by History, which carves the Universe into discrete series. In this case, after the Revolución Libertadora, there was no possibility of the series beginning again. People used to tell the eminently poetic story of a letter delayed in the post, which reached its addressee years later (long after 1955) with the Evita stamp, like starlight reaching the earth long after the extinction of the star. Finally, Marta pronounced a sentence that summed up their endeavor and gave it meaning: "It's all we can do for her, poor thing." Their dear departed had bequeathed them the task of completing the collections, but at the same time, Evita, who had died too, was imposing a task of her own. The sentence made an impression on me, and I rushed off to repeat it to my mother, word for word. "Filthy Peronists," was her reaction. This was an instance of the world turned upside down: the Peronist middle class. But since the world encompasses everything, there is also a place in it for life in reverse, as in the case of the dead father.

My friend L seemed to be living proof of the legend in which each boy was his mother's son and each girl her father's daughter ... This wasn't really a legend; I think it was my personal interpretation. What people said was that sons resembled their mothers while daughters resembled their fathers. I took this in a literal and exclusive way: since we were all boys, fathers in general became redundant. That must be where I got the idea that my father was a bigamist; he had no choice, if he wanted to fulfill his reproductive function. And whatever the neighborhood witches said, it didn't contradict his devotion to the Virgin, because it was She who epitomized solitary motherhood of the Son. To fit with the story, the man of the house had to make himself scarce and become a stranger. Maybe my father was referring to this curious condemnation when he spoke of "life in reverse." Or not. Maybe he was thinking of the path that he had to follow back through time to find me, the son lost in the mother. But I'm rambling. All my life I've been trying to understand that simple, lapidary formula: "life in reverse." I've explained it in a thousand ways, and none of them entirely convinces me.

"Life in reverse" also makes me think of those little creatures that live (or sleep) suspended from the branches of trees. It's an inhuman existence (maybe that's what my father was talking about: inhumanity), but only, of course, when considered from a human point of view. Animals are different from us; they have a different history, biology, and chemistry. To speak of their "customs" is already a human projection.

There was a rather poetic episode (though it made me look like a little fool) involving the strangest of those creatures: the bagworm moth. They don't seem to exist anymore. Perhaps they have become extinct; it seems entirely plausible, almost inevitable. Not because of attempts to control or eradicate them, which were totally ineffective (when have humans ever been able to overcome a plague?), but because the creature itself was too complex and improbable to triumph over time. It was a kind of fat worm, the size of a finger, which surrounded itself with a little conical basket woven from twigs and pieces of leaves. It made itself indestructible. Whenever I tried to undo the basket I failed because it wasn't just woven but stuck together with a glue secreted by the creature itself, a glue so adhesive that it turned the cocoon into a single mass. The worm was never visible; it never left its cone, suspended from the branch of a tree. Did it hang head down or head up? Who knows? Until the events that I'm about to relate, I had always thought that those creatures chose a place and stayed there all their lives: a natural supposition, because they were more vegetable than animal.

I have already mentioned the fireplace in our room. From time to time we used it, not for heating (we were never cold) but for burning things. The chimney drew perfectly; no smoke or odor came into the room, and that must have been why my father bothered to set the fire—for the pleasure of using something that worked well—because he could just as easily have burnt those things (dry leaves, trash, old bits of furniture) on a fire out in the garden, where there was plenty of space. Maybe, though, now that I think of it, he had an unconscious desire to do everything in *our* space, within the microcosm that was legally ours to inhabit.

Another symptom of that desire: he kept his ladder under the bed—as if there weren't twenty-four empty rooms in which he could have stored it—and at least half its length stuck out, so we had to be careful not to trip over it. One Sunday my father took out the ladder and spent a long time removing bagworms from the top of a tree in the garden, the one closest to our door. He pulled them off, threw them down onto the ground, then raked them up into a phenomenal heap.

"Now what?" I asked.

"Now we're going to burn them."

He took them inside to the fireplace in a bucket, making a number of trips. When they were all inside, he ordered me, in his curt and nervy way, to finish the job, because he had something else to do.

"Don't worry, Dad! I'll look after it," I said as I went to get the matches. He left, as if in a great hurry, without even glancing back at me. I heard the bicycle squeaking as he wheeled it along the gallery, and then, in the distance, the front gate opening. Where could he have been going? I returned pensively to the fireplace. Burning a mountain of bagworms might seem a strange and cruel task, but it was the most appropriate mode of destruction for those dry, crackly creatures.

I too must have had something to do, because I simply struck a match and tossed it onto the heap, then left. I must have been in a tremendous hurry, because I didn't even stay to see if they caught fire. This explains my show of diligence, my "Don't worry, Dad": I was impatient to get rid of him. Mom wasn't at home. The house remained empty all morning. At midday, I was playing in a vacant lot around the corner when I heard my mother crying out, calling me home for lunch. She had a high, piercing voice, and didn't hesitate to make the whole neighborhood resound with my name if she needed me, even for the most trivial reason. I could hear her several blocks away. When I got home, my father was waiting for me at the gate. We went in together. I must have suspected that something was wrong, because the first thing I looked at was the fireplace. It was clean and white: not a single bagworm. I thought that they must have cleaned away the ashes and were cross because I hadn't done it myself. I began to mumble an excuse, but a sixth sense warned me that it would be better to keep quiet. We ate our lunch in silence. The atmosphere was poisonous. I was thinking: "Is it really that bad? Can't they forgive me?" I went to lie down on my bed.

Then I saw them. They were all on the ceiling, hanging from the white plaster, way up high, unreachable. They had occupied the whole surface, spreading themselves out, leaving each other the living space dictated by their instinct. But it wasn't an even spread; there was a denser surge, a kind of Milky Way. It was an amazing, unforgettable spectacle. All over the ceiling ... like little Chinese lanterns ... they had escaped and climbed up there in search of altitude.

I was filled with the most abject terror. Not for one second did I think that my parents might not have seen them. And yet they hadn't looked at them once, or referred to them in any way ... I sat up on the bed. Mom was washing the dishes; Dad was still sitting at the table, listening to the radio. Were they pretending? Were they waiting for me to start screaming? I didn't stay to find out. Luckily I hadn't taken off my shoes; my bad habit of flopping onto the bed with my shoes on—Mom was always scolding me for it—turned out to be providential. I made a beeline for the door, passing within inches of my father's back … He would only have had to stretch out his arm … but he didn't: it was as if he had disowned me. I opened the door, shut it behind me without turning around to look back, and started running madly down the gallery, toward the street … It was as if I would never return. I was leaving them behind like two funereal statues … I was fleeing. I felt that I was fleeing toward my own death.

I was no stranger to the experience of flight: burning my ships, leaving it all behind and plunging into the unknown, starting over from scratch, building from the ground up, beginning a new story … It's true that I had very little to abandon, but children cling to whatever they have all the more tightly because they still haven't made it entirely theirs; they're still discovering its secret mechanisms. Yet I was prepared to throw it all away at the first sign of danger.

So I fled … as I always did. But I didn't go far. I never went far because I never left the neighborhood. No one ever stopped me, or even noticed, probably; I was always within two or three hundred yards of home. I knew that territory by heart, and it was sufficient for me. Its utterly familiar mysteries held my dreamy young soul in thrall. When my mother took me to the town center, I went enthusiastically but then I forgot all about it; impressions made by the rest of the world had no purchase on me.

There were certain details of the neighborhood, important for my games, that I must have been the only one to notice. For example, the angle at which the buildings were cut away at the corners ... I knew the configuration of every corner by heart, from playing one of the games that I had invented, the one that I called "the corner game," or, to be more precise, "the *little* corner game." The diminutive was a way of expressing the game's secret, intimate, intraconscious nature, its function as a joke or puzzle for others and a private source of fun for me.

Having reached this point, I realize that I need to describe the little corner game, or explain it (in a case like this, description *is* explanation). In fact, I have been meaning to do this for some time, although I'm slightly embarrassed about expanding on something so childish and pointless. Still, if I don't do it, no one else will, and the knowledge will die with me, and who can say what might turn out to be important for somebody else? My hesitation may also be due to the difficulty of explaining a mechanism at once so precise and so futile.

As I said, the game was played within the limits of my consciousness, and I played it on my own, although at the expense of others. Opportunities arose by chance, although I did sometimes help to set them up. The basic situation was this: I would be walking along in the street and notice that someone was walking behind me, in the same direction, either on the same sidewalk or the opposite one. The other person could be a grown-up or a child, someone I knew or a stranger, anyone at all, although, in fact, I knew almost all of my victims, more or less. I would keep walking at the same pace until I reached the corner and then I would turn. As soon as I was hidden from view, I would sprint until the moment at which I calculated that the person behind me was about to reach the corner, and then I would resume the pace at which I had been walking originally. So when my victims saw me again, I would be inexplicably far away, and they would ask themselves, "How is that possible?"

I'm using the term "victim," but it was obviously a very mild form of victimization. Setting aside the distracted types who didn't even notice, at most I led people to doubt the testimony of their senses, or shook their confidence in the soundness of their reckonings and predictions. The joke would have been consummated perfectly if my victims had feared that they were losing their minds, or better still, if they had started to panic about a subtle crumbling of the laws of physics, as if on reaching the corner they had stepped into a world with a different spatio-temporal paradigm. I don't think anyone had such an extreme reaction. It was a harmless enough little game, although the motivation behind it was undeniably cruel. I assumed the role of the "malicious demon" postulated by all the philosophers.

The game had its technique, which I took very seriously. For a start, when walking "visibly," before and after the sprint, it was necessary to maintain a constant pace, as slow as possible without attracting attention: normal, natural. And the sprint had to be as fast as possible. I also had to restrain my urge to start running before I had completely turned the corner and was entirely out of view, which meant that I had to gauge exactly the angle

of the cutaway. I had learned from experience that the merest
hint of an intention to run, the slightest tensing of muscles, was
a giveaway, even from behind and at a distance. I had to do the
opposite: relax and imagine that I would go on walking at that
leisurely pace for a long way. Naturally, the most difficult thing
was calculating the moment at which the other person would
reach the corner; this was the calculation that the victim would
perform in turn, erroneously. I couldn't afford to make an error; to be seen running would have been embarrassing, so, in
fact, I would slow down a bit before the anticipated moment,
just to be sure; I sacrificed a little "trick distance" so as not to
run any risk. It's important to remember that the whole game
was played "blind": the other person was behind me, and at no
point did I turn around to look back, because that would have
given me away.

I wonder if this description really makes it clear. The ideal
account would be a series of diagrams: schematic maps of the
streets and the corner, indicating the trajectories of the moving bodies but also the victim's lines of sight: broken and dotted
lines could be used, respectively, and little crosses with letters
(A, B, A′, B′) to mark the positions at various moments in the
game. Fundamentally, it was a map game.

The odd thing is that in spite of my precautions, and even
when it all went to plan, everyone detected the trick—that is,
they realized that there *was* a trick, that it wasn't natural (or
supernatural, which is what I wanted to make them believe).
And they saw what the trick was. If they were kids, they yelled

out straightaway: "You didn't fool me! You ran! Did you think I wouldn't work it out?" and so on. If they were grown-ups they kept it to themselves, but sooner or later they would let me know. Certain ladies, mothers of my friends, whom I had thought would be easily fooled, would put me on the spot later on, asking why I had run away from them. That was how adults saw it, in general; they couldn't grasp the pure fun of a gratuitous practical joke.

I said before that everything is allegorical. In a way, this little game is an allegory of life. It could serve as a diagram to illustrate the aspirations of young people in small towns. All the fantasies of escape, success, and return conform to the same basic scheme; they all revolve around the transmutation of the inquisitive hometown gaze. That merciless gaze, which turns the town into a prison, is what the young hope to escape from above all, but only to recover it with a vengeance, years later, as a witness to their transformation.

"Years later ..." That's where the trap lay, in that little phrase, essential even to the most dazzling success. Because years later one would be an adult, and the gains in terms of professional success, money, and fame would be matched by the increase in size, and the figure wouldn't seem so far away. The years would neutralize the career.

It's incredible how important, and how insistently present, biological time is in small towns of the kind that are said to be "frozen in time," which do indeed have a chronology of their own. It's something people think about, the object of constant calculations, never far from consciousness. It provides a link between children and adults. Even the most respectable and well-intentioned adults are always using the theme of age to communicate with children. On one occasion, I remember, the reasonable man who had been holding forth in the accountant's office about the education of the young raised the subject with me. He asked how old I was; I told him. Let's suppose I was eight.

"Eight? You've had your eighth birthday?"

"Yes."

"Then you're nine." I must have looked puzzled, because he went on to explain: "You've completed eight years and you've started your ninth. But if you don't go into details, and nobody's asking you to, you have a perfect right to say, 'I'm nine.' You've already celebrated your eighth birthday, so the eight years are done already, and now you 'are' nine." He gave me a conspiratorial wink; maybe he was secretly anxious to ensure that I'd followed his reasoning. I wouldn't have disappointed him, because I was quick on the uptake, and this question of age was something that mattered to me as a small-town kid. Even so, he repeated himself to make sure that I had grasped his meaning. It was important to him; and no doubt he was systematically spreading this bright idea like the Good News in all his conversations with the local kids.

It didn't have much of an impact on me, because I had begun to lose sight of the future; increasingly, my life was limited to the present, in the form of my immediate surroundings. I could hang out in the street all day while remaining within the circular range of my mother's voice: I think I was always hoping, or fearing, that she would call me to announce some urgent news, some portentous revelation. That expectation created an inviolable present from which I didn't even dream of trying to escape. I had become very sensitive to the inherent fragility of the family unit. I wanted to "be present" when things happened, not so much because I was curious or a busybody, and certainly not because I thought that my presence could avoid a catastrophe, but because I had convinced myself that unless I saw it with my own eyes, no one would be able to give me a proper account of what had happened. I suspect that I was also vaguely afraid of running into my father's "other family" in the unfamiliar parts of town, a prospect that filled me with horror, I don't know why.

The next step, which I duly took, was to turn back to the past. Not as nostalgia or history, but in a constructive, optimistic spirit. The project was born, predictably, on the day of my first excursion beyond the limits of the neighborhood, or the first that left a memory, an experience that I can recount. This happened when I was ten or eleven. It was a Sunday morning, the morning of a Sunday in spring. There was to be a ceremony on the Plaza, on the other side of town, beyond the center, to inaugurate the Monument to the Mother, and our teacher had suggested that we attend. There was some powerful incentive; I think she had told us that we would have to write an essay about it on Monday. My mother approved of the idea and dressed me in my best clothes. I set off with two boys who lived across the street, also in their Sunday best. Many people were heading in the same direction, to go to mass as well as the inauguration: the church faced onto the Plaza, and on Sunday morning there were three masses, at seven, nine, and eleven. My friends, including those two boys, went to mass, but I didn't, of course. The ceremony on the Plaza was to take place between two masses. The occasion was momentous because this was to be the first statue in Pringles. Although the town was a hundred years old, it didn't have a single statue. Until then, no one had felt the lack … A few years earlier, a monument had been inaugurated but it was abstract. The Monolith, as it was known for want of a better name, was a kind of squat obelisk (it would have been about nine feet tall), made of bricks and plaster. It was at the intersection of Boulevard 25th of May and Boulevard 13. In Pringles, the streets had names and numbers: they all had numbers, but only the ones in the center had names as well. Those central streets were always referred to by their names; their numbers remained hidden, reserved for mapmaking purposes; and where the names gave out, toward the edge of the town, the streets were known by their numbers, while waiting to be baptized. In this case the two intersecting streets were of different status, but the one that had a name had the name of a number, or a date, to be precise. The Monolith had been donated to the town by the Rotary Club; it was very simple and geometrical, but it bore the strange symbols of a secret society.

Even so, no one would have called it a statue, so the Mother had no precedent: no one could dispute her inaugural condition.

When we were about fifty yards from the Plaza, two boys from school rushed up to greet us. Apparently they had been waiting on the corner for some time, anxiously looking out for anyone they knew, and they had been too impatient to stay put and let us cover that last stretch on our own. They came running as fast as they could and started trying to tell us something while they were still a ways off . . . but they were prevented from speaking by uncontrollable bursts of laughter; they were choking, unable to finish a word. We smiled uncomfortably; we wanted to share their joy but we didn't understand. Meanwhile we kept walking toward the Plaza and gradually we realized that the cause of the laughter was the statue, which was right there, very close to the corner. They dragged us toward it, still in a frenzy of hilarity, "cracking up," tantalizing us by gasping, "You'll see," between guffaws.

The statue itself was a total anticlimax. It seemed old hat, even to me, although I'd never seen a statue in my life. It was a mother nursing a baby, slightly larger than life, on a very vulgar pedestal of red granite. The figure was made of white cement cast in a mold, or so it seemed, mainly because of the classic pose, just like something you would see on a postage stamp. There were quite a lot of people in that part of the Plaza and on the opposite sidewalk in front of the church, but no one was paying attention to the statue, and to judge from the tricks that our laughing friends had played, no one had been keeping an eye on it.

Just at that moment, however, a family stopped to look at the Mother, and our guides were obliged to champ at the bit, although they could barely restrain their impatience. Meanwhile, they managed to indicate what the joke was ... It was hard to grasp, not just because laughter kept interrupting them, but also because the joke itself was too ineffable to be communicated in words; it was one of those things that you have to experience to understand (and that, precisely, was why they wanted to try it on us). Apparently, they had climbed onto the pedestal and had pressed on the Mother's nipple with a finger while saying, "Koo-koo," or along those lines. That was it. There was no need for more, because it was infinitely funny. The laughter ... the same laughter that choked them and bent them double when they tried to tell us about it ... came surging up automatically, unstoppably ... "Koo-koo" ... the funniest thing in the world. "You'll see!" It was unbelievable; or rather, you had to see it to believe it ... Which explained their enthusiasm, the excitement with which they had gone to the corner to wait for us, or anyone they knew, so that they could share this marvel. Like all discoverers, they were bursting with impatience to divulge the new worlds that they had brought to light. They had made their discovery by chance, playing a silly joke, for no reason, but that is how the great discoveries are made.

In the end the bothersome onlookers moved on. Agile as a monkey, one of our friends jumped up onto the red granite

and put his finger exactly on the nipple, saying, "Koo-koo" …
To our immense surprise, nothing happened. He tried again:
"Koo-koo." Then he tried with the other hand, changed his
posture, got a firmer footing, tried again … A powerful magic,
perhaps the same one as before, but inverted now, prevented all
laughter. Even our smiles were beginning to fade.

"That's so weird," he said, looking at the other boy, who was
equally puzzled. "You try …"

He got down, yielding his place. The other boy climbed
up but without conviction: something was telling him that it
wouldn't work; and sure enough, when he put his finger on the
spot and said, "Koo-koo" — nothing; the machine had broken
down. It was like a decree of fate, and that was just why they
couldn't accept it; they racked their brains trying to find an explanation.

"How come … I don't know what's going on … Just a moment ago … we touched the nipple …" But there was nothing to be done: even talking about it was no fun anymore. The
laughter had gone flat. I suggested that we wait a while to see if
it would recharge. They didn't even listen to me. The situation
had become vaguely ridiculous; to go on trying would have
been to enter into an infinity of disgrace; the statue itself was
taking on a depressing tinge.

We split up. I wanted to go for a walk, to get some sense of
what, for me, were virtually new surroundings. It was a spring
morning, as I said before, sunny and perfect. Suddenly, having extricated myself from the infernal machine of the Mother,

I had plenty to see. The Plaza in Pringles is one of the most outstanding architectural complexes in the country: it's Salamone's masterpiece, and he was one of those geniuses whose legacy grows in value with the passage of time and successive generations.

Francisco Salamone (1897–1959) was schooled in the modernist style. He studied in Córdoba and was an engineer as well as an architect. In 1936, Governor Fresco, a conservative leader with regal schemes and vast financial resources, commissioned Salamone to design and construct public buildings in the province of Buenos Aires, and seems to have given him carte blanche to realize his projects. In less than five years of feverish activity, city halls, abattoirs, and cemeteries were built in Pellegrini, Guaminí, Tornquist, Laprida, Rauch, Carhué, Vedia, Azul, Balcarce, Salliqueló, Tres Lomas, Saldungaray, Urdampilleta, Puán, Navarro, Cacharí, Chillar, Pirovano, and Pringles. The designs are dominated by a blend of art deco and Mussolinian monumentality, but there are traces of other styles as well: Assyrian and Egyptian, futurist and oneiric. In a few cases, the design is not limited to the building but takes in the surrounding landscape or cityscape, and the most fully achieved of these larger projects is the one that Salamone executed in Pringles. The Plaza occupies two blocks; in the large, central oval stands the biggest and most beautiful of all Salamone's town halls. The stylistic motifs of its colossal mass are repeated in the Plaza's lamps, benches, pergolas, and fountains, as well as in the paving on the sidewalks. The artist also oversaw the tree planting: rare species from the far south were used; according to local legend, they have since become extinct in their places of origin and survive only in Pringles. The elegant linden trees in double rows bordering the sidewalks around the edge of the Plaza were an exception to this exoticism.

Scholars have pointed out that Salamone's highly coherent design, with its far-reaching formal correspondences, which create a kind of continuous spatial story, and the make-believe inventiveness of its style, foreshadowed the development of theme parks, the first and most famous of which would appear in California many years later. So you can imagine my astonished awe as I rediscovered this wonder on that Sunday morning. Slim, red carp circulated in the fountains, suspended in invisible water. I stared at them for a long time, and when I looked up at the square tower of the town hall, I felt that so much beauty was impossible to bear.

I began to remember ... I had been there before. Of course I had ... I used to go there often; it was my favorite outing. But so long ago ... When you're a child, you measure time differently. What is a distant memory for a child of ten? There is no room in such a small life for the great expanses of nostalgia, so I could only think of it as having occurred in another life. But in my mind the concept of "another life" was subject to a powerful taboo because of its hidden meanings, so I made it "the same" life, my one and only life, which acquired strange dimensions, stretching away into the unknown ... That was how I began to value the possibilities of the past: it was an inviolable strongbox where all my secrets were safe, a virtual cave where I could pile up endless treasures and keep them there at my disposal, simply waiting to be fetched. In a climax of empowerment, I felt that even the monster Amnesia, with its utterly unpredictable form, could fit into that elastic container. And to serve as Ariadne's thread or the trail of bread crumbs, to stop me getting lost, there was Style: Style was the very substance of the Plaza.

I was beginning to recognize my surroundings, and reconstruct the circumstances that had taken me there in another time.

I had been very young: three, or four ... It was before I started school. My father would bring me on his bicycle, balanced on the crossbar, between his arms. A simple calculation revealed that this must have been during his time as council electrician, when he was in charge of the street lighting. Which meant that he would have been too busy for such outings with his son (still a new toy) except on Sundays, and specifically on Sunday mornings, because in the evenings he would have had to switch on the lights: there were no days off for them. Those earlier visits, then, had taken place on the same day of the week, at the same time of day. This repetition accentuated the Plaza's eternal character; and it seemed highly significant that I had returned, for the first time, just when the Monument to the Mother was being inaugurated, since this was the first interference with the site's artistic unity, although it was discreet: the statue was in a corner, hidden by a beautiful blue spruce ...

And why had my father gone there on Sunday mornings?

One thing opened out into another (that's the beauty of memory). By answering that question, I could specify the time more precisely: the Sundays that I was remembering had been in spring. Memory was bringing me infinitesimally closer to the present ... My father came to collect the linden tree's little flowers, those starry yellow clusters with which we used to fill a bag. I set off on one of the sidewalks, with its borders of blue and white paving stones arranged in a zigzag pattern, and felt that I could see myself, years before, in exactly the same place, trotting along behind my father, tottering on my chubby little legs, holding the bag, eager to help, as always ... He wasn't a tall man but he could reach the lower branches without needing the ladder, which he didn't bring on those excursions. The lindens were small, almost miniature trees — I had since grown tall enough to reach the leaves myself — but on those first visits they must have seemed enormous.

At the time, my father must have seemed enormous too, a giant. But a good giant: I followed him around, seeking his protection. Although his nerves were always on edge, I didn't feel threatened by his angry outbursts, perhaps because they weren't directed at me. We were still in our father-and-first-child "honeymoon." Perhaps he had not yet dismissed the idea of having other children. Peronism was still in flux, still protean: it hadn't yet settled into a definitive form. And I can't deny that he was in an unusual position. He'd had the courage to marry — for love — a woman who wasn't normal. And not only that, he had dared to procreate, to assume "the charge" of a child. Anything could have emerged from my mother's womb: a monster, for example. Waiting through her pregnancy must have been a torment for him; maybe that was what ruined his nerves. I turned out to be normal, but risking it a second time, playing the genetic lottery again, with such risky numbers, would have renewed his fears. It was a difficult decision. Also, given my tender age at the time when he was bringing me to the Plaza, my normality would still have been subject to confirmation. Babies, by their very nature, are in a sense little monsters; I might have turned out to be a dwarf or to have needed spectacles ... Perhaps that was why he took me out on the bike and kept me by his side whenever he wasn't working: to observe me. I was human plasma, unpredictable and protean, like Peronism. Then the years went by, and I grew up normally, and the Revolución Libertadora put an end to the possibility of giving me a brother or a sister.

All that seemed so far away, so different ... What had happened? How could we have changed so much, if everything was still the same? It all seemed too much the same, in fact. I felt nostalgic for time itself, which the Plaza's spatial stories made as unattainable as the sky. I was no longer the small child who had gone with his father to collect linden blossoms, and yet I still was. Something seemed to be within my grasp, and with the right kind of effort, I felt that I might be able to reach out and take hold of it, like a ripe fruit ... So I set out to recover that old self.